A Candlelight Ecstasy Romance

"MARSHA, I WANT YOU TO BE MY WIFE."

I was afraid of this, Marsha thought as she stared into Ward's earnest face. "Are—are you sure?" she stammered. "Marriage is such a big step. Wouldn't you rather live together first?"

Ward shook his head. "Marsha, you're not the type and neither am I. I want to marry you."

Oh, no, what could she say? Sorry, Ward, I can't trust my own judgment? I'm scared because I love you so much? She smiled and gave Ward's hand a squeeze. "If you honestly think that I'm what you want, then I'll be glad to be your wife."

"Yes, you're what I want, purple bras and all," Ward assured her.

"I guess we'll have to finish the champagne." Marsha laughed as Ward filled a cup for her.

"I guess we will. To us!" he said, holding his cup to hers.

"To us," she replied. Oh, Ward, she thought, I hope I'm right—this time. . . .

A CANDLELIGHT ECSTASY ROMANCE®

A
MATTER
OF JUDGMENT

Emily Elliott

A CANDLELIGHT ECSTASY ROMANCE®

Published by
Dell Publishing Co., Inc.
1 Dag Hammarskjold Plaza
New York, New York 10017

ISBN: 0-440-15529-0

Printed in the United States of America

First printing—July 1984

To Our Readers:

We have been delighted with your enthusiastic response to Candlelight Ecstasy Romances®, and we thank you for the interest you have shown in this exciting series.

In the upcoming months we will continue to present the distinctive sensuous love stories you have come to expect only from Ecstasy. We look forward to bringing you many more books from your favorite authors and also the very finest work from new authors of contemporary romantic fiction.

As always, we are striving to present the unique, absorbing love stories that you enjoy most—books that are more than ordinary romance.

Your suggestions and comments are always welcome. Please write to us at the address below.

Sincerely,
The Editors
Candlelight Romances
1 Dag Hammarskjold Plaza
New York, New York 10017

CHAPTER ONE

Marsha Walsh rinsed her hands at the sink and turned around to help her very pregnant young patient sit up on the examining table. Joan Pruett smoothed the sheet around her swollen stomach and grinned tiredly. "So it won't be this week?" she asked wistfully.

Marsha sighed sympathetically. "Frankly, it doesn't look like it," she replied. "You haven't dilated any yet, although there are signs that may start soon. But don't get discouraged, Joan. Sometimes, with a first baby, we're still surprised by an unexpected arrival."

"But probably not, right?" Joan persisted doggedly. Joan was a math major at the university and was used to dealing with the black-and-white world of numbers, not the unpredictable world of new babies.

"Probably not," Marsha agreed.

"Oh, damn!" Joan wailed. "I'm so sick of being pregnant I could scream."

"Poor Tom," Marsha said dryly, a twinkle in her eyes.

"Yeah, I'll probably go home and take it out on poor Tom," Joan agreed. "I never dreamed that the last month would take this long."

"The last month always drags," Marsha said soothingly. "But I do have a suggestion for you. Go out to eat at least twice this week and see a movie or two. Not only will it pass the time for you, but it will be your last chance to do those things for a few months." Frugal Joan opened her mouth to protest, and Marsha held up her hand in warning. "I mean it. Get out and have a little fun while you still can. Now, are you going to do that or do I call Tom and give him instructions?"

A small grin played around Joan's mouth. "We'll go," she said as she slid off the table, the sheet still wrapped around her body. "Thanks, Miss Walsh."

"See you next week, Joan," Marsha said warmly as she shut the door of the examining cubicle behind her. Glancing down at Joan's chart, she remembered that Joan had requested a home birth and she made a mental note to check her bag tonight just in case Joan's baby did the unpredictable. Her bag was probably all right, but she hadn't checked it since the home birth last week, and she wasn't sure she still had enough suture. Shaking her shoulder-length blond hair away from her face, she wandered into the small office that she shared with Laurie Rodriguez, the other midwife who worked with Dr. Neimann. Although Marsha and Laurie practiced from the same office and covered for each other on alternate weekends, they seldom saw each other, since they had different office days, Laurie seeing patients on Tuesdays and Thursdays and spending the rest of her time with her family, and Marsha seeing patients on Mondays, Wednesdays, and Fridays and working the other two days of the week at Planned Parenthood as a counselor. Marsha kicked off her shoes and made her calls, then completed and filed her charts, longing for the day when she and Laurie would be able to hire a secretary. Although they were doing pretty well, nurse-midwifery was just catching on in Austin and it would be at least a few more months before they would be able to afford a full-time secretary.

Marsha sped through most of the charts and filed them

10

quickly, but she stared at the file of one of her new patients as a frown flitted across her forehead. She reread the file carefully, then stood up and headed down the small corridor to Hal Neimann's office, ignoring the way that Dr. Neimann's last patient stared at her stockinged feet. She stuck her head around the corner as Hal shook the hand of a drug salesman and ushered him to the door. The salesman brightened and smiled warmly at Marsha, receiving her sparkling grin in reply. She ducked in under the salesman's arm and sank gratefully into the soft overstuffed chair that Hal kept to one side of his desk. Hal promised the salesman that he would look through the brochures that he had left and prescribe the samples to some of his patients, then turned around and shut the door, smiling at Marsha tiredly. Worn out as he was, he was still appealing, and Marsha knew, had he not been married, her attraction to him might have led to something. "Just what I needed at the end of the day," he said ruefully.

"Why didn't you tell him you run a natural childbirth office?" Marsha teased. "No drugs of any kinds. A little herb root, but that's all. That would have gotten rid of him in a hurry!"

Hal laughed out loud. "Yeah, and I can just see the reaction that I would get at the next County Medical Association meeting if it ever got out," he replied, knowing that, as it was, some of the other doctors considered his liberal views on the matter of childbirth positively peculiar.

Marsha laughed with him, warming to the sight of his tired face relaxing. "Some of them couldn't believe it when you set up shop with Laurie and me. Here," she said abruptly, shoving the file she had brought with her under Hal's nose. "She wants to come to me, and she wants a home birth. What do you think?"

11

Hal picked up the chart and studied it. The woman was in her middle thirties and had had two previous uncomplicated deliveries. But her blood pressure was a bit on the high side, and her blood sugar was a bit above normal too. Since nurse-midwives were trained to handle only normal, uncomplicated deliveries, any patient who had a complication that might become a prenatal problem was encouraged to use a regular obstetrician and deliver in the hospital. Hal scratched his head and studied the chart. "Is money a problem?" he asked. He and the midwives served a fairly affluent group of patients, but occasionally a patient wanted a home birth in an effort to save money.

"Didn't appear to be," Marsha replied as she wiggled her toes in Hal's carpet. "She said that she didn't like the sterile hospital atmosphere." And that she wanted the personal attention, Marsha added to herself. Although Hal and the other OB's did the best they could, they simply did not have the time to devote to each patient that the nurse-midwife did. "I explained to her that the blood pressure and the sugar were not danger signs, but that they might indicate a potential problem and that she might be better off with you, so I said I'd talk to you about it, and she agreed to abide by our decision."

"Well, I think you can go ahead and take her on," Hal said as he shut the file and handed it back to Marsha. "Just watch her like a hawk, and if either of those conditions gets any worse, we can co-supervise the pregnancy or I can take her if I have to. But if I take her on, she'll have to go into the hospital for the delivery." Although Hal was pretty liberal about most things, he still insisted on a hospital or birthing center delivery.

"She seemed reasonable," Marsha said as she stood up. "Are you ready for Easter?" she asked wickedly as she glanced at the picture of Hal's two little boys on his desk.

"Sandy's about got that taken care of," Hal grinned. "The boys are getting a live rabbit this year."

"That sounds like Sandy," Marsha said with amusement. Hal's pretty wife was well known for her love for small furry creatures.

"And I got a little something for Sandy's Easter too," Hal said as he stepped over to the wall safe and spun the combination. He popped out a small box and opened it. A beautifully faceted pink stone winked back at them, shimmering even under the fluorescent lights.

"What is that?" Marsha breathed. "Surely not a diamond that color?"

"Good Lord, no. I couldn't begin to buy her a diamond this size. It's a pink tourmaline. I bought it to go with her pink dress." Hal shut the case and put it back into the safe.

Marsha sighed wistfully at both the necklace and the thought that had gone into finding it. "Sandy will love it," she predicted confidently.

"I hope so," Hal grinned. "And at least she won't have to change its paper! See you Wednesday, Marsha," he said as he sat back down in his chair to return his calls.

" 'Night, Hal," she said as she gently shut the door to Hal's office and filed her new patient's chart. Marsha sat down and called the woman, informing her that she would take her on with the understanding that if things did not go well, Dr. Neimann would be called in. Then Marsha removed the jeans and shirt that she had stored in the closet and wandered toward the small bathroom to change her clothes. She didn't mind her uniform during the day but disliked wearing it after hours.

"Have a date tonight, dear?" Mrs. Gilbert asked as Marsha walked past the back door to the receptionist's office.

"Sure don't," Marsha replied as she shifted her clothes

to her other arm. Mrs. Gilbert was a sweetheart, but she missed mothering her own children, who had probably fled from home as soon as it was humanly possible, and she lavished her motherly attention on everyone in the office, from Hal on down. It grated on Marsha's nerves, but Mrs. Gilbert was too nice a person and too good a receptionist to offend by asking her to lay off. "I'm going out with my sister Amy for supper."

"Oh, yes, that little professor who was in here last week," Mrs. Gilbert replied. "I swear, she's the most fragile little thing I ever did see. She'll never have that baby normally, as little as she is."

Marsha stifled an outburst of laughter. That "fragile little thing" hadn't missed a day's work since her pregnancy had been confirmed, and Marsha's examination had found Amy surprisingly roomy internally for the normal delivery of even a large baby. "Oh, I think she'll do fine," Marsha said soothingly.

Mrs. Gilbert shook her head. "But she works too hard. You both do. Why, look at you, no bigger around than a matchstick. I bet you're just worn out every afternoon when you get out of here, aren't you, dear?" she clucked sympathetically.

"Not really," Marsha replied, not adding that she usually either took her bicycle for a ten-mile spin or skated around the neighborhood for an hour or more once she left work. That would leave Mrs. Gilbert a perfect opening to expound on the dangers of a girl riding alone on the city streets.

"Well, I'm making a German chocolate cake this evening, and I'll bring you in a piece," Mrs. Gilbert said firmly. "You simply have to get a little more meat on your bones. And you can take that little bitty sister of yours a piece too. Such a tiny thing, she is," she carried on as Marsha ducked into the bathroom. She locked the

14

door behind her and quickly shed the white uniform that she wore in the office, leaning back to stare at her figure in the full-length mirror that she and Laurie had installed as an incentive to their patients to control their weight. Yes, she was as slender as Amy, but where Amy did indeed look fragile, Marsha's figure had a taut energy that radiated from her small curves and gave her body an electric sensuality that fascinated members of the opposite sex. High, firm, small breasts spilled out of her minuscule bra, and her lacy bikinis did little to hide her flat stomach or gently rounded bottom. No, she definitely did not need any more meat on her bones, she thought as she slipped into a western-cut shirt and rolled up the sleeves almost to her elbows. She stepped into her new tight jeans and sucked in a breath to zip them, then pulled on open-toed sandals. Reaching into the small cabinet, she pulled out a washcloth and washed her face, then reapplied her blusher and lip gloss. She stood back and cocked her head to one side, staring at her face in the mirror. Analyzed feature by feature, her face was not exceptional, with a little too much nose and a wide, curving mouth, but when the features were put together and enhanced with the right makeup, the effect was dynamite, and even she realized it. More striking than pretty, she turned men's heads wherever she went. I wonder why, she mused. Maybe it's the eyes, she thought as she ringed them lightly with a blue liner that matched her gleaming irises. Or the hair, she thought as she dragged a brush through the thick blond mane that fell in a smooth curve to her shoulders. Or maybe it was just her smile, the one that made her sparkle.

Oh, well, what good has it done me? Marsha asked herself as she tiptoed by Hal's door to collect her purse and the beeper. Luckily, Mrs. Gilbert had left for the night, and Marsha did not want to interrupt Hal's conversation just to say good night. Besides, he was in a hurry to get home to Sandy and the boys. Grabbing her purse, Marsha let herself out the back door of their suite and wandered down the hall to the elevator and punched the Down button. Emerging into the lobby, she headed for the employee lot and located her old red and white Monte Carlo, promising herself a new car soon after she hired a new secretary. She sighed as she spotted Hal's sports car in the next row.

Damn, she thought sourly as she pulled out of the parking lot, why are all the good ones already taken? Hal was kind, decent, reasonably good-looking, and very, very married, Marsha thought as she stopped for a red light at a busy intersection. Hal was crazy about Sandy and didn't even look the other way. And it's not just him, she said to herself as the light changed and she drove through the busy downtown traffic. All the good men are snapped up by the smart girls, Marsha thought, while the rest of us are out there screwing up.

Willing her thoughts elsewhere, Marsha drove through the rush-hour traffic and onto the University of Texas campus. The large, sprawling campus housed one of the most prestigious universities in the nation, and Amy had been quite honored when she had been invited to spend a year working on a joint project with some of the other top malacologists in the country. Amy's small university in San Antonio had willingly granted her the year off, and her husband had practically worn out his Datsun running back and forth to his business in San Antonio so that Amy could take the position. Marsha had moved to Austin about the same time and had been delighted to find herself in the same town as Amy for the first time since Amy had graduated from high school and left home twelve years before. Marsha drove through the shady campus, grinning at couples kissing in the grass and

16

dodging the Frisbees littering the drives, and parked in a visitor's space in front of the biology building. She entered the huge, labyrinthine building and loped down a flight of stairs into the basement. Peering into Amy's office and finding it empty, she wandered across the hall and stuck her head in the door of a large, messy laboratory, spotting Amy sitting cross-legged near piles of carefully sorted mussel shells. On the shelf above Amy's head was a row of bottles, each labeled with a year, month, and lake, and full of preserved specimens. Amy picked up a shell, carefully examined it, then tossed it into a particular pile. "There you go, you little stinker you," Amy muttered as she stood up awkwardly and rubbed her aching back. "Ouch!" she exclaimed as she brought her hand up to her swollen stomach. "Do you have to poke those sharp little feet into my stomach, little Patterson?" she grumbled as she brushed off the seat of her denim pants.

"Don't you dare talk to my niece or nephew like that!" Marsha admonished her sister, laughing as Amy stuck out her tongue. "You'll warp his psyche. Children need lots of love, you know."

"I love him a lot better when he isn't kicking me in the gut." Amy smiled sweetly, flinching when the baby kicked her again. "Sorry, little one. I won't gripe about you," she added, patting her stomach gently. "How long have you been here?"

"I just got here," Marsha replied as she took in the row of bottles on the shelf. She knew that Amy and the other scientists were dissecting the mussels month by month, determining when each species reproduced. Then, so that normal reproduction was not hampered, they would time the application of the compound that Amy had perfected to combat the effects of a serious parasite that had almost wiped out the Central Texas mussel population several years ago. Above the table Amy had mounted some of her husband's photographs of the mussels in various states of dissection and micrographs of the parasite that had done such damage. "Are you ready to go?" Marsha asked as her stomach growled loudly enough to be heard across the room.

Amy picked up a bottle and extracted a mussel, expertly slitting apart the muscles that held the shell together. "Would you believe I need to go through at least half of these bottles tonight?" she asked as she ran her fingers through her short, stylish hair.

"Go through them? Let's just cook them and be done with it," Marsha laughed as she peered over Amy's shoulder.

Amy opened the mussel and gently moved aside some organs with her tweezers. Spotting something, she grabbed the bottle and read the date again. "August? I don't believe it! No way you're cooking this one, Marsha. This little baby was gravid when we picked her up. This is the first lead we've had."

"Gravid?" Marsha asked.

"Yeah. Pregnant. Just like me," Amy replied as she plunked the mussel back into the jar. Rubbing her back, Amy made a note on a pad beside her and reached for another mussel in the jar. "Marsha, would you hate me if I backed out on dinner tonight? The others are waiting for me to get this done, and we need it by tomorrow if I can."

Marsha smiled understandingly. Amy had not come out and said so, but she was probably the only scientist of the group who could readily identify the gravid mussels. But it would be child's play for Amy, the South Texas malacological expert and a virtual genius. Amy's career had taken off like a rocket from the beginning and had soared even higher with the publication last year of her second book, her first actual text. "Of course I wouldn't

18

hate you, although how you can condemn me to an evening of my own cooking is beyond me," she complained ruefully.

Both women laughed at Marsha's reference to her lack of culinary skills. "Well, if you're that desperate, I'll call Rick and have him bring some greasy tacos from S.A.," Amy said as she grinned wickedly.

"All the way from San Antonio?" Marsha said as she made a face. "They would be as cold as ice. Seriously, is Rick coming in?"

"Not until tomorrow," Amy said as her face softened at the mention of Rick's name. "He's coming with me to your childbirth class, remember?" She smiled gently at the thought of her husband.

He's really made her happy, Marsha thought wistfully as Amy opened another mussel and fingered its insides gently. Marsha had been frankly doubtful when Amy had married the big, good-looking photographer, thinking rather narrowly that Amy would have been happier with a fellow genius. But Amy had blossomed in the year and a half that she and Rick had been married, and she had clearly made him happy too. And then, what do I know about picking men anyway? Marsha asked herself rather cynically. Her brilliant older sister had chosen her man well. Marsha cast admiring eyes on Amy. Yes, Amy had done well, both in her profession and in her private life.

"Listen, I'll leave you to it then," Marsha said as she gave her sister a quick hug. "Don't stay too late and get overtired, all right? Remember, you are seven months pregnant," she added firmly.

"Yes, Mother," Amy said dryly.

"I'm speaking professionally, you understand," Marsha said as she wagged her finger at Amy. "See you tomorrow!" she said as she galloped out the door and ran right into the hard, warm body of a man who was trying to come into the laboratory. Not expecting to be hit by a flying woman, the man lost his balance and toppled to the floor. Marsha stumbled and fell on top of him, finding herself staring into a pair of warm brown eyes that were laughing up into her startled face.

"S-sorry," Marsha mumbled, blushing to the roots of her hair as the man smiled up at her. The impact of his closeness left Marsha stunned as she struggled to roll off him. The man's face was classically handsome, with beautifully molded bones that stopped just short of being too perfect. High cheekbones, a square chin, and a strong jaw combined with a straight nose to turn Marsha's legs and arms to jelly and thus further complicate her struggles. His mouth was curved into an intimate grin with only a hint of wickedness lurking at the corners. And he had a dimple in his left cheek just at the corner of his mouth. Marsha felt the involuntary quickening of the beat of her heart in response to the nearness of this appealing stranger, and she was strangely loath to do anything that would remove her from the intimate position in which she found herself with him.

The man reached out with two strong arms and grasped Marsha around the waist, lifting her off him. Recovering the use of her legs, she made contact with the floor with the soles of her feet, standing up quickly as he let go of her waist. "I—I'm sorry," Marsha stammered again as she extended a hand to help the man up from the floor. Was it her imagination or did he hold her hand for just a fraction longer than necessary?

"No harm done," the man said as he smoothed the ruffled brown hair on the back of his head. Although Marsha in the past had always been drawn to blond men or redheads, she experienced an unfamiliar urge to reach up and run her fingers through the thick brown mane that he was trying in vain to straighten. Although profes-

20

sional styling might have helped a little, the man's hair was the thick, wiry kind that did pretty much what it wanted to, not that Marsha found it unattractive in the least. If anything, this hint of imperfection only added to the man's charm.

As she stared up into his smiling good-looking face, she found herself wondering who he was and why he was going in to see Amy. Stifling an unexpected urge to return to the laboratory on an invented pretext, she smiled her sparkling smile at him and turned around to leave. "Excuse me," the man said suddenly. Marsha turned around hopefully. "Do you know if Dr. Patterson is still here?"

Marsha hoped that her face didn't mirror her disappointment. "She's working in there," she said, pointing toward the open laboratory.

"Ward, is that you?" Amy called through the open door.

"Coming, Amy," he said as he grasped Marsha's arm and propelled her through the open door. Baffled, Marsha made no protest as the man steered her to the lab table where Amy was fingering the insides of yet another mussel. "I just got run over by this madwoman out in the hall and thought she might be a student of yours."

Amy's face split into a grin as she looked up and saw Marsha blushing furiously. "So you're at it again, Marsha," she said dryly. "No student, Ward, this is Marsha, my sister."

"Your younger sister, I presume?" Ward asked as Marsha smiled broadly and Amy shot him a look that could kill.

"Yes, klutzy li'l old Marsha just bowled him over," Marsha replied, recovering her sense of humor, although her heart was still beating unaccountably fast. "You must forgive me," she said to Ward, deadpan. "I fall over my

21

own two feet on occasion. No one else is safe in the vicinity."

"Oh, but I've never been bowled over by a lady before," Ward replied gallantly. "It was my pleasure. I'm Ward Sentell, by the way. I'm working on the same project as the rest of these brainy clowns around here."

"Come here then, Bozo, and look at this," Amy commanded him. "I have an August gravid here—a Cyrtonaiasis. I've never seen that before."

"That's because Cyrtonaiasis is a Mexican species. They reproduce at a different time of year from the other species."

Ward and Amy continued their conversation. Although much of it was beyond the range of Marsha's knowledge of mussels, Ward was obviously as knowledgeable on the subject as Amy was, and Amy seemed to respect his opinion highly. Marsha wondered why she had never been introduced to Ward before. Amy had been on the project for almost eight months, and at one time or another Marsha had met nearly everyone associated with it. As the conversation continued for a number of minutes, Marsha tried to slip away surreptitiously but found that Ward was still holding her arm gently but firmly and that she could not easily extricate herself from his grip. Finally, as the hunger pangs began to torment her stomach in earnest, she tapped him on the arm and looked at her trapped wrist pointedly. "If you'll let go of me, I'd like to go home and feed my face."

"Sorry," Ward said unrepentantly as he loosened his grip on her arm but continued to hold it lightly. The touch of his fingers was sending a light shiver up Marsha's arm, making her aware of the sensual strength of his fingers.

"Better let her go and find herself some food, Ward,"

22

Amy admonished him. "She was supposed to go with me and I let her down. I have to get this done by morning."

"Well, why don't I take you out for a bite then, Marsha?" Ward asked, running one finger up the inside of her wrist in a feather-light touch.

Immediately, the usual warning bell went off in Marsha's head. "No, I d-don't think so," she stammered quickly, her refusal an act of self-defense. It was one thing to be attracted to a stranger and flirt with him a little, another to actually go out with him.

Ward's face fell. "Really, I'd love to take you out for a bite. I'd stay with Amy if I could be of any help to her, but she's the only one of us who can identify the gravid stage by sight."

Marsha looked into his smiling, eager face, tempted beyond belief to go, yet terrified to do so. He was so good-looking and seemed so nice. Yes, that was it. He was too nice. With a guy like this one, there had to be a catch somewhere. She started to shake her head again but caught Amy out of the corner of her eye giving her the thumbs-up sign. Well, if he had Amy's seal of approval, he must be all right, she thought gratefully. "All right, if you don't mind going with me in jeans, I'd love to go out for dinner with you," she said with charming candor, flashing Ward a smile that made him catch his breath.

"That's settled, then," Ward said as he slid his hand up Marsha's arm and steered her toward the door. "Don't stay too late, Amy," he called as he and Marsha walked out the door together. As they climbed the steps to the front door of the building Marsha sneaked a look at her impromptu escort for the evening. He was tall, even taller than her ex-husband, Jerry, and her head barely came up to the top of his shoulder. He was thin but well-muscled, with strong, tan arms extending from the short sleeves of the western shirt that he wore. Although his grin was

23

boyish, telltale lines around his eyes and his mouth gave his age away as somewhere in his middle thirties. His arms and face were unusually tanned for the middle of April, and since it was really too early to begin the ritual of sunbathing, Marsha wondered how he had gotten the dark tan. He looked down and smiled at her winningly as they approached the top step, and reached in his pocket. "Penny for them," he said as he handed her a bright shiny penny.

"How did you get so tan?" Marsha asked frankly.

"I spent the winter on a motorboat," he replied as he put the penny into the pocket on her shirt front. His fingers lightly brushed her breast through the soft fabric, and Marsha felt her nipple knot in response to his fleeting touch. She sucked in her breath tightly and hoped he did not notice the way her body had responded to his fingers.

Marsha opened her mouth to ask him about the boat, but Ward had crossed the hall and was speaking to the security guard stationed at the front door. "Dr. Patterson is working in lab 120," he said to the guard. "She's down there alone and I know everybody on the project would appreciate it if you'd keep an eye on her this evening."

"Will do, Dr. Sentell," the man promised him with a grin.

"That was nice of you to ask him to keep an eye on her," Marsha said as they walked out the door.

"Well, she'll be down there alone and she is pregnant, even if she doesn't let it slow her down," he replied.

"Oh, the baby isn't due for a couple of months yet," Marsha said blithely. "And she's healthy as a horse."

"Better leave a statement like that to a professional," Ward said as he steered Marsha toward the visitor parking. Marsha started to protest that she was a professional, but her attention was diverted by Ward's groan. "Damn, I forgot. I'm on my motorcycle."

"We can go in my car if you trust my driving," Marsha said as she pointed toward her car. She unlocked the doors and Ward opened the door on the driver's side for her, then got in on the other side. "Where would you like to go?" she asked as she put the car in gear.

"From the sound of your stomach, somewhere close and fast," Ward said dryly as Marsha's stomach rumbled again.

"How about Howard's?" she asked, referring to a small hamburger bar and grill on the edge of campus that was known for their assemble-them-yourself burgers. "That is, if you don't mind running into a few of your students there."

"Fine with me, if you don't mind running into a few of your professors."

"My professors are all in Waco and Dallas," Marsha said dryly. "I'm not a student."

"And my students are all at New Mexico State," Ward replied smoothly.

"So you're not a regular professor? I should have known that," Marsha mused as she dodged a small dog that ran out in front of the car. "Profs don't get that kind of tan," she said by way of explanation when Ward's eyebrow shot up. She parked in front of Howard's and they walked into the noisy hamburger emporium, waiting in line until the youthful cashier took their order. The boy handed them their beers and they wandered through the restaurant looking for a vacant table. Finally they spotted one on the glassed-in patio, far enough away from the juke box to allow for conversation. Marsha sank gratefully into a chair and sipped her beer greedily. "Ah, this is bliss," she murmured as she licked the foam from her lips. "I missed lunch today. Had a noon delivery."

"What did you have to deliver?" Ward asked humorously as he sipped his beer.

25

"A nine-pound boy," Marsha said absently as she sipped her beer again.

"A baby?" Ward asked incredulously. "You delivered a baby today?"

"Of course," Marsha said, baffled at his reaction. "I deliver at least three a week."

Ward looked at her face and did some swift mental arithmetic. "Either you were a child prodigy like Amy and got your M.D. when you were a baby yourself, or you're the youngest looking thirty-year-old that I've ever met. No wonder Amy gave me a dirty look."

Marsha laughed out loud. "Wrong on all counts. I'm twenty-six, younger than Amy and older than I look, which I don't mind one bit, thank you! Definitely not a child prodigy, although I will admit to a cum laude after my degree. And although I guess I'm old enough to have an M.D., I'm not old enough to have gone through residency or to have a full-fledged obstetrical practice."

"So how do you manage to deliver three or more babies a week?"

"I'm a midwife," Marsha said simply as she licked a drop of beer off her finger.

Ward's face wrinkled into a frown of concentration. "A midwife? I've heard something about that recently, but I thought that went out two generations ago."

"It did," Marsha said frankly. "But it's made a big comeback in the last few years. Although there aren't too many of us yet, there is a growing demand for our services."

At that moment their number was called over the loud-speaker. Ward and Marsha retrieved their hamburgers at the counter and took them, naked except for the bread and meat, down the table that had all the condiments spread out on it, so that the diners could doctor their hamburgers to their own personal satisfaction. Marsha smeared hers with mustard and mayonnaise, then piled it high with lettuce and tomato, topping it with a small ladle of melted cheese. She noticed that Ward limited himself to slices of tomato and two ladles of the jalapeño cheese. The top of his head's going to be sweating by the time he finishes with that burger, Marsha thought wickedly as she remembered the one and only time she had tried the jalapeño cheese.

They claimed another beer each and headed back to their table. "So tell me more about your career—I'm fascinated," Ward admitted as he took a bite of his burger. His eyes widened and watered suddenly, but he valiantly chewed and swallowed the bite he had taken. He immediately followed it with a large mouthful of beer.

Marsha took an enthusiastic bite of her burger and swallowed it hungrily. "I'm a midwife—a nurse-midwife, actually," she said as she took another bite and ate it gratefully. Ward eyed his hamburger doubtfully, then took another bite and swallowed it quickly, swiftly following it with another generous portion of his beer. "I'd get a glass of water if I were you," Marsha said sagely.

Ward signaled a busboy for a glass of water as Marsha continued. "I have my own practice, just like a doctor, and I provide prenatal care and deliver the baby. If the mother wants me to, I'll follow the baby for the first month or two, but after that the baby goes to a regular doctor. I also provide a certain amount of well-woman care and until my practice is full-time I moonlight two days a week at Planned Parenthood, helping women with their birth-control needs." She took another bite of her hamburger and noticed that the sympathetic waiter had brought Ward two glasses of water. Fortified by the water, Ward ate his hamburger, one small, cautious bite after another.

"How on earth did you get into a field like that?" Ward

27

asked. "I mean, I thought everyone but the very poor went to a doctor."

"Well, nurse-midwifery did start out that way," Marsha admitted. "In the early days of the specialty, long before I ever got into the profession, the nurse-midwife did serve mostly the rural poor, or she delivered in areas where a regular doctor was not available. But recently, the middle class and affluent types are getting interested in using a midwife. In fact, very few of my patients are poor."

"Very interesting," Ward acknowledged as he nibbled on his hamburger, accompanying it with frequent gulps of water. "But why would a woman who can afford a doctor use a midwife? I'm not criticizing, I just want to know," he added candidly.

"Well, her motivation isn't financial in my case," Marsha admitted. "I charge almost as much for a delivery as Dr. Neimann. He's my consulting physician, and he writes all the prescriptions for my patients and takes them if the delivery requires surgical intervention," she added, as Ward looked puzzled. She cocked her head to one side thoughtfully. "I think that the reason most of my patients want to use a midwife is that I can provide them with much more personal care than a physician. Although I charge as much as a doctor, I don't carry near the case load, and then, although I'm limited to what I can do by the amount of training that I've had, I can also provide a lot of services that the average doctor can't, or won't, provide. I can provide a home birth, if that's what my patient wants, or deliver her in the birthing center. I can spend an hour with her on her first visit to me, and I can spend thirty minutes on a subsequent visit if she needs or wants me to. I'm there with her through much of her labor and can coach her and help her through the rough spots. I don't just arrive at the last

28

minute with the bucket to catch the baby," she added wryly.

"You provide much more personalized care, it sounds like," Ward said thoughtfully. "Seems great to me. How about you? What do you get out of it besides your living?"

"Are you kidding? Do you know what a great feeling it is to help a new life into the world?" Marsha's eyes snapped and unconsciously widened in delight.

"Can't say that I do, but I'll bet it's just wonderful," Ward said softly.

"Oh, it is," Marsha replied fervently, delighted that Ward could understand her pleasure in her chosen profession. She ate the last of her hamburger, reached for her beer, and picked up the mug, then realized that it was empty.

Ward grinned sheepishly. "Sorry," he said ruefully. "That jalapeño was hot!" His lopsided grin made Marsha's heart do a funny little thump in her chest. Good grief, what a delightful man! Where had he been hiding for the last eight months?

"I've been doing field research," Ward said blandly.

Realizing that she must have articulated at least some of what she was thinking, Marsha blushed furiously. "Field research?" she asked quickly to hide her embarrassment.

"I've been making all the collections in the lakes and rivers around the state and bringing the specimens back to the campus for the rest of the think tank to work on," he explained. "Although I've worked more closely with Amy than with anyone else on the team. That woman has a mind in a million."

"Yes, she does," Marsha said in complete agreement.

"And I'm really looking forward to sitting down and writing all this up with her," he added. "My field work is finished for the most part. We just have to sit down and make sense of the data. Hey," he said suddenly. "I bet you're delivering her baby, right?" he asked.

"Sure am," Marsha acknowledged proudly. "Wouldn't miss it for the world."

"But I am going to get after Amy," Ward said seriously. "She has mentioned a sister from time to time, but I had no idea she was related to a knockout like you."

Marsha blushed at the compliment. Had it come from another man, she would have dismissed it as just a smooth line. From Ward, though, the sentiment seemed sweet and sincere. Maybe he really did think she was a knockout! Although their conversation over dinner had been anything but provocative, there was an undercurrent of awareness between them, not tension exactly, but a potent attraction that pulsated between them. Boldly, in spite of the blush, she looked him straight in the eye. "Thank you," she said honestly. "I'm sorry I didn't know about you sooner too."

"So let's make up for lost time," Ward said genially as he stood up. "Would you like to go dancing tonight for a little while?"

Marsha looked down at her jeans and shirt. "Western dancing," Ward amended. "We're both dressed for that."

The warning bell went off in Marsha's head again, but this time she ignored it firmly. Ward seemed very nice, and she most definitely did want to go out dancing with him. "Name your dance hall," she said as she licked a crumb from a finger. "Sounds great to me."

CHAPTER TWO

The dance hall they selected was a converted bowling alley on the edge of town. Ward offered to take Marsha to a fancier place but she refused because of their casual dress. Besides, she liked the band that was playing, a local band that was extremely good, and in a few years it would probably make the big time. The bored cashier took their cover charge and stamped their hands, then Ward took Marsha by the hand and led her into the cavernous, dimly lighted dance hall. The crowd, large for a weeknight, was either dancing on the large, concrete dance floor, playing the videogames that lined the walls, or sitting at the folding tables that ringed the dance floor, drinking beer and swapping tall tales. Ward stopped at the refreshment booth and bought a beer for himself and a Coke for Marsha, and they threaded their way to an empty table on the opposite side of the room, close to the small bandstand. They sat down and Ward popped open the beer and drank a little, although he did not seem to be as uncomfortable from the jalapeño as he had been earlier.

"It's been ages since I've gone western dancing," Ward volunteered. "How about you?"

"Oh, not that long," Marsha admitted. "Although it was with a group, not a date." She bit her lip, wondering why she had volunteered that last bit of information.

"Looking over the local stud population, huh?" Ward teased as Marsha blushed furiously, looking around the room and spotting a number of drugstore cowboys prancing around in their tight jeans and their new boots, hoping to make a conquest.

"Most of the local studs are a little young," Marsha said dryly. "They have a way of wandering back to the dorms after the dance hall closes." Although it was true that many of the men in Austin were very young, there were a number of graduate students and teaching assistants nearer her own age that she could have dated if she had wished to.

The band struck up a lively Mel Tillis number. Marsha, who loved western dancing with a passion, felt her toes twitching under the table. Ward looked over and grinned wickedly. "Want to try this old man out?" he challenged.

Marsha jumped up and they headed for the dance floor. As soon as they reached the edge of the floor, he took her into his arms and led her into a lively two-step, holding her firmly but leaving them plenty of maneuvering room so that they would not be kicking each other's legs. He twirled Marsha around the floor with the practiced ease of someone who had spent many a Saturday night in a dance hall like this one. Marsha, no slouch herself, matched his steps perfectly, and they moved together with the grace usually found only with partners who had danced together a long time. The number was long, and they were both breathless by the time it was over. At that point the band broke for a short breather, so they headed for their table and drank from their cans gratefully.

"That band is good!" Ward exclaimed sincerely.

"I figured you'd like them once you heard them," Marsha said as she sipped her Coke. "I've heard them before, and they're always a treat. I wouldn't be surprised to see them hit the big time. So how about you? Where did you learn to dance like that?"

Ward grinned sheepishly. "Saturday-night dances around Karnes City," he admitted. "I'm a country boy." He looked at her shrewdly. "How about you? Where did you learn to dance like that?"

Marsha laughed ruefully. "Dance halls on the outskirts of Waco and Dallas. I'm a city girl. I cheated."

Ward laughed out loud at her admission. "Oh, well, at least you know how to have a good time," he teased. "What were you doing in Waco and Dallas?"

"College and nurses' training. I got a B.S.N. from Baylor, which meant two years in Waco and two in Dallas. I went back later for my midwifery training and got that in Mississippi."

"Why so far away?" Ward asked. "Couldn't you have gotten it closer to home?"

A shadow passed across Marsha's face that Ward couldn't help but notice. "I needed to get away from things about then," she said quietly. "And, too, the school is excellent."

"I've missed dancing in the last few years," Ward said quickly in an effort to take Marsha's thoughts away from whatever painful subject he had unwittingly brought to mind. "They have a few dance halls in New Mexico, but I haven't had time to go often. I'd forgotten how much fun it can be with the right partner." He smiled softly and Marsha warmed with delight. So she was the right partner to dance with. Although it was a simple compliment, she felt warm and happy in a way that she hadn't experienced in a long time.

The band filed back up on the bandstand and tuned their instruments a little, then broke into a lively Willie Nelson number. Ward and Marsha rose in unison and hurried to the dance floor, moving again into the simple yet intricate pattern of the two-step. When that number was over, they launched into an old-fashioned rock-and-roll tune that Marsha thought they would have to sit out, but Ward confidently led her through it, although she had never danced much rock and roll before. They whirled and twirled, Ward whipping her under his arm and back around, the other dancers, clearing a little space around them to give them room. Marsha was sputtering and breathless by the time the dance was over.

"Whew, maybe we better sit the next one out!" she exclaimed as the number came to a close.

"No, let's dance it," Ward said as the band went into a dreamy ballad. He pulled Marsha into his arms and held her tightly against him. Trapped against his warmth and unwilling to escape, Marsha gave herself up to the dreamy dance, savoring every moment of being in Ward's arms. His breathing was deep and his pulse was rapid from the fast dancing, and Marsha could feel the thudding of his heart in his chest. Her own breathing was ragged, her pulse pounding, although it was excitement, not exertion, that was making her body behave in this fashion. This close, she could smell Ward's crisp aftershave mingling with the musky odor of his body, and her sensual feelings, which had long been dormant, awoke with a clamor and demanded to be heard. Marsha could feel desire curl in the pit of her stomach, and it was all she could do to keep from reaching up and curling her fingers into Ward's wayward hair and lifting her mouth to his. Her breasts pressed against Ward's chest, and desire flowed through every part of her body. The warning bell went off in her head again, but she ignored it firmly and gave herself up to the pleasure of being cradled in Ward's arms. They danced slowly, swaying with the music, savoring the pleasure of each other's touch. When the dance finally ended they parted reluctantly, each loath to break the contact that had been so stirring.

"All right, all you lovers, break it up out there and get into formation. It's the cotton-eyed Joe!" the lead singer called from the bandstand.

Ward grinned as he reached around and grasped Marsha by the waist. "This is all right, but I liked the other kind of dancing better," he admitted as she twined her arm around him and the band swung into the cotton-eyed Joe. Ward and Marsha faced the same direction and fell into the circle of dancers that was forming on the dance floor. Another couple joined them, Marsha holding the man's waist although not as closely as Ward's, and together they joined the roomful of dancers kicking and strolling their way around the dance floor. There was a good deal of laughing, and shin-kicking, and stumbling around the circle, but luckily the couple who had joined with them were fairly good dancers and had not had too much to drink, so the four of them were able to move around the circle fairly gracefully, hopping and stomping their way through the lively dance.

As the band came to the roaring conclusion of the dance, the lead singer leaned into the mike. "Now, since you're already in position, let's do a cumbia!" he called.

"What on earth is that?" Ward asked, his brow wrinkled in puzzlement.

"It's a Mexican dance," Marsha said as the other couple broke away. "Actually, it's easier than the cotton-eyed Joe." Ward watched the dancers for a minute, then grasped Marsha's hand, and they entered the circle of dancers again, strutting to the lively beat of the music.

Ward and Marsha danced for several hours, even though it was a weeknight. They danced the lively numbers with great relish and clung to each other during the slow dances, savoring the closeness that those dances per-

35

mitted them. Finally, Marsha looked at her watch and gasped. "My God, Ward, it's after midnight!" she exclaimed. "I have to be in the office by nine."

"Oops," Ward said as he grasped her wrist and read her watch, sending shivers up her arm with his light touch. "I guess we better go." He took her hand and together they made their way to Marsha's car. They tried to make small talk on the way back to the campus, but the sensual tension, which had been building ever since Marsha had plowed into him, was taut and hampered their attempts to speak. The attraction was deep and potent, sending all reason from Marsha's mind and filling it instead with a deep desire to touch Ward, to kiss him, to feel his sensuous mouth against hers. Ward's fists were clenched in his lap as though it were the only way he could stop himself from touching her while she drove. Marsha drove onto the campus, deserted now except for an occasional pair of lovers kissing in the moonlight, and found the parking lot where Ward's motorcycle was parked. She pulled up beside it and turned to Ward.

Her thank-you was crushed in her throat as Ward lunged across the seat and grasped her by the shoulders, bringing her face close to his and kissing her with hungry urgency. Marsha met his embrace willingly, unable to make even a token protest as Ward plumbed her mouth to the depths. Her fingers leapt to the springy mass of hair that she had longed to caress all evening, and she wound her fingers into the unruly curls at his nape, finding them surprisingly soft to the touch. Ward snaked one arm around her shoulders and pressed her in the center of her back, forcing the points of her breasts nearer the hard wall of his chest. With his other hand he gently stroked back the soft blond mane. Gently removing his lips from hers, he rained down soft kisses on her cheeks and even lower, nibbling her neck and earlobes, teasing

36

the two small studs she wore in each ear with his tongue. Gasping, reeling from the sensuality Ward was arousing, Marsha boldly ran her hands down his back, feeling the ridges of sinewy muscle running the length of his back and into the waistband of his jeans. Returning his lips to hers, he gently ran his tongue across her teeth, gasping in the embrace when Marsha opened her teeth and teasingly tangled her tongue into his. One hand dipped daringly and caressed her breast through her thin shirt. Unconsciously, Marsha thrust her breasts closer to his erotic fingers, at the same time eagerly exploring his hard chest with a gentle touch of her own. The sensual storm that had been building all evening was being unleashed in all its fury, and Ward and Marsha were powerless to stop it, not that either of them wanted to.

Finally Ward broke off their kiss and slowly they moved apart. "We better call a halt, or we're going to be in your backseat," he said in an uneven voice.

Marsha nodded, shaken by the force of the emotion that this man had aroused in her. No man, not even her ex-husband, had ever made her feel this way, and she was frankly stunned by Ward's impact on her senses. What would making love with him be like? Involuntarily, Marsha swayed toward him, and he took her face in his hands and kissed her long and lovingly, then set her away from him and held both of her hands in his. "I'll call you, all right?" he asked softly.

Marsha nodded. "Thanks for the evening," she said quietly, her face shining and her hair tousled from the embrace they had shared. She watched as Ward got out of her car and walked to the motorcycle, kicked it into gear, and roared out of the parking lot. She raised a hand to her lips, still throbbing from Ward's sensual possession, and touched them gently. Good Lord, she thought, no one's ever done this to me before, made me feel like this. Marsha smiled into the darkness. No, Ward made her feel like no man had ever been able to before, and darned if she didn't like it!

Ward turned under the overpass and took the entrance ramp to the expressway. That woman's dynamite, he thought as he relived their torrid embrace in the car. Never in his thirty-four years had he been so moved by a simple kiss. He had had to literally drag his hands off her to keep from making love to her right there in the front seat of her car. He was grateful for the cooling, calming effect of the wind whipping his face and his body as he brought his motorcycle up to speed and roared down the expressway toward his home in a subdivision on the outskirts of town. As it was, he needed a cold shower, and he doubted that he would get much sleep tonight.

Tearing his mind from their kiss, Ward thought about the rest of the evening. Marsha had been a wonderful companion, just as he had told her she was. She had danced like a dream, and she had been a lot of fun to talk to. And what an unexpected profession! She didn't look like the type of woman who would go into that demanding a career, yet she had and she apparently loved it. And I'll bet she's good at it, he thought. I'll bet her patients just love her.

A small frown clouded Ward's face as he remembered that she had not wanted to go out with him at first. She had been distinctly wary and would have refused altogether if Amy had not signaled something behind his back. I wonder why she hadn't wanted to go, especially when she had so much fun once she had gone. Had someone hurt her at one time or another? Oh, well, at least she had gone. And from the way she had kissed him, he was sure that she would go out with him again.

Ward eased his motorcycle from the expressway and

headed down the side street to his ranch-style home. It's late, he thought. I hope Katy didn't wait up for me again. He turned the corner and pulled up into his own driveway, noting with satisfaction that the lights were all off, except for the front light. I guess I should have called and made sure that Katy was all right, he thought ruefully as he wandered up the sidewalk. I wonder if Katy knows about midwives? He promised himself that he would ask her tomorrow morning at breakfast.

Marsha woke to the sound of the telephone jangling in her ear. She came swiftly awake, long months of getting calls at odd times conditioning her to instant wakefulness in case she was talking to a mother in labor. "Marsha Walsh," she said crisply, sitting up and reaching for the pen and pad by her bed.

"Mornin', doll," a familiar voice drawled in her ear.

"Jerry, damn it, it's six forty-five in the morning," Marsha snapped into the receiver. "What do you want?"

"Ah, I see that spinsterhood is not agreeing with you, dollface," he replied exuberantly. "Want me back?"

"Go to hell, Jerry," Marsha replied dryly, more exasperated than angry. Although they had been divorced for nearly two years, she heard from Jerry every other month or so, usually at odd hours, and the bitterness she had felt while they were married had faded to a dull pity for him and disgust with her own former lack of common sense. She knew she should probably refuse to even talk to him, but the softer side of her nature would take pity on him every time, and she would find herself listening to Jerry, sympathizing with him and offering advice and encouragement.

"Sorry I woke you," Jerry said a little sheepishly. "I forgot about the time difference."

"Where are you now, Jerry?" Marsha asked.

"Miami Beach. I got a job as a bartender in a brand-new hotel. The boss says that I have a lot of potential and that I have a good future with his hotel chain," he babbled eagerly.

And how many times have I heard that one before? Marsha asked herself. The sad part of it was that the man had probably said just that to Jerry and meant it. Jerry was bright, he was personable, he was easy to get along with, and he probably could have a good future with the hotels if he would only keep the job long enough to find out. But he wouldn't. It might take one month, maybe two, or even three if the job was extra exciting, but Jerry would become bored and go off chasing another big chance, another rainbow. In the two years that they were married Jerry had held seven jobs, none for more than a month or two. He was always searching for the instant path to success, never content to work his way to the top. Sighing as memories flooded back, Marsha gripped the receiver. "That's wonderful news, Jerry. When do you start your job?"

"Tomorrow," Jerry said enthusiastically. "And, Marsha, you don't know how excited I am. This is the big one, I just know it."

Sure, she thought, just like the real estate scheme in Tennessee last winter, and the job in Las Vegas before that. "That's wonderful, Jerry," she said with as much enthusiasm as she could muster. "How's Felicia, by the way?"

"Oh, I'm not with her anymore," Jerry said lightly. "She didn't want to come to Florida."

You mean she got tired of supporting you, Marsha thought cynically. But she couldn't really blame the girl for getting fed up. Hadn't she? "By the way, Jerry, now that you're working, do you think you could pay me back the money that you owe me for the lawyer's bill?" she asked dryly.

"Su-sure thing, Marsha," he stammered. "But better yet, why don't I send you a plane ticket to Florida and we can have a vacation together, just like the old times?" Jerry made his voice properly nostalgic.

Here it comes, Marsha thought. The let's-get-back-together speech. The we-had-so-much-going-for-us speech. Jerry came up with this one every time he was between girlfriends. Fortunately, at that point the beeper beside her bed went off, the sharp *beep* followed by the usual garbled message. "Sorry, Jerry, got to go. My beeper just went off. Call me when you have the money you owe me," she added wickedly.

" 'Bye, love," Jerry replied, not mentioning the money again.

That jerk will never change, Marsha thought cynically as she dialed the number of her exchange. I'll never see that money. Although the sum was not large, it still rankled her that Jerry had had the gall to borrow his lawyer's fee for the divorce from her, and that she had been stupid enough to lend it to him. Her exchange gave her the number to call, and Marsha dialed Joan Pruett's number. "Joan, this is Marsha Walsh. You're having contractions? How far apart are they?" Marsha laughed out loud. "I'll get my bag and be right there. I told you that first babies surprise us sometimes, now, didn't I?"

Marsha ran a brush through her hair and dabbed on a little lip gloss, stopping to touch her lips with the tip of one finger. Her full lips were even wider than usual, a little swollen from last night's torrid kisses from Ward. Had she really kissed him like that? Was his mouth still tingling from the pressure of hers? Smiling to herself, she pulled on a pair of jeans and a T-shirt that said MIDWIFE

41

in bright pink letters. Tonight she was going out to eat with Amy and Rick, and then they were going to attend her prepared-childbirth class that all of Marsha's patients were required to attend, a series of six classes to prepare themselves for the physical and emotional experience of childbirth. Marsha enjoyed teaching the classes, since she got to know her patients even better during the sessions, and her patients were able to cope much better with labor and delivery after some training.

Marsha was pulling on her shoes when the doorbell rang. She grabbed her purse and answered the door, finding herself engulfed in a huge bear hug from her brother-in-law, Rick. She returned his hug and invited him inside. "Where's Amy?" she asked.

"Over at the lab," Rick replied easily. "We're supposed to pick her up in a few minutes. So, Marsha, how's the baby business? Are the June brides keeping you busy?"

"That was last month," Marsha cracked. "This month it's all those July vacation babies." She turned out the lights and shut the door behind her.

"And in June it's all those torrid Labor Day weekends," Rick quipped.

"So that's what happened," Marsha said dryly as Rick helped her up into his van. "I didn't think Amy was planning a baby just yet, even though it didn't seem to bother her when she found out."

"And that's where you're wrong," Rick said as he switched on the motor and backed out of the driveway. "As crazy as it sounds, we planned this baby even though we knew we would be doing the long-distance routine." His face softened as he thought about his pregnant wife. "I'm not sure which of us wanted this baby more," he said quietly. "I just hope everything goes well."

"I'm sure it will, Rick," Marsha said confidently. "She's a model pregnant lady, and she's done fine up to

42

this point." She smiled to herself. Although Rick was the picture of confidence in front of Amy, in private he tended to fret and had come to Marsha more than once for a little extra assurance that everything was going well. Knowing how crazy he was about Amy, Marsha did not mind providing the extra reassurance.

Rick and Marsha chatted about various things on the way to campus. In spite of her initial doubts about Rick as a husband for Amy, Marsha had become very fond of the big, good-looking man, and she was sure that the affection was returned. He had been delighted when he learned that Marsha would be living in Austin, because it meant that Amy would have some family close by. Never having experienced that kind of concern from Jerry, Marsha admired Rick for his concern about his wife's well-being when they had to be apart. Marsha, in fact, admired Rick for a lot of reasons. Coupled with his love for Amy was a witty sense of humor, and Rick could have both Marsha and Amy reduced to blushes in a matter of seconds with his outlandish comments that were funny but never unkind. Yes, Marsha thought, Amy has a winner here. But, then, maybe I met a winner, too, she thought as they pulled up in front of the biology building, remembering the passionate kisses she had shared with Ward in the same parking lot.

Amy was sitting on the steps of the building, waiting for them. When she saw the van, she got up awkwardly and walked over as Rick jumped out and lifted her in and Marsha scrambled through the space between the seats, sitting on a jump seat in the back. Amy sat down in the seat Marsha had vacated and smoothed her blouse over her stomach. Rick got in on the driver's side and kissed Amy warmly, running his hand halfway down her stomach before jerking it away in surprise. "Little stinker kicked me," he complained.

43

Amy kissed Rick again, then pulled away. "We better stop this," she muttered. "Might get in trouble this way. My mama always told me . . ."

Rick and Marsha broke out into guffaws of laughter. "Amy, it's too late!" they sputtered in unison.

Amy looked down in feigned surprise. "You mean it isn't the chocolate cake?" she asked innocently.

"Oh, come on," Marsha said. "Feed me supper. I'll teach you all about it later."

They laughed as Rick started the engine and headed for Amy's favorite restaurant. While Rick and Amy got caught up on the news from San Antonio, Marsha laid her head back and thought about her sister. Marsha had wanted a marriage like Amy's, warm and loving and mutually supportive, and although she had become discouraged as of late, she hadn't given up the dream.

The small restaurant that Amy liked served Chinese food, and the three of them ordered different entrees so they could share them and sample three delicious dishes. As the waitress left with their orders, Amy turned to Marsha. "Did you have a good time last night?" she asked a little too casually.

Marsha looked at Amy and smothered a laugh. Amy was dying to know what had happened after she and Ward had left her. "Would you believe nothing?" Marsha ventured, teasing Amy with her reticence.

"No, I would not," Amy replied firmly.

"Didn't think so," Marsha admitted. "Would you believe that we went to Howard's for hamburgers?"

"Yes," Amy said. She drank a sip of her water and fiddled with her wedding ring. "And?"

"We went dancing," Marsha said. "Western dancing."

"And?" prompted Amy.

"And what?" Marsha asked innocently, dragging out the torture.

"And what? Did he kiss you? Are you going out again? Do you like him? Are you . . ."

"Amy!" Rick exploded. "For crying out loud, what business is it of yours?"

Amy turned innocent eyes on Rick. "I introduced them," she said simply. "Well, Marsha?"

"Marsha, I guess you better tell her," Rick sighed exasperatedly. "She'll badger you until you do."

Marsha laughed out loud. "All right. Amy, he has to be the nicest guy I've met in a long time. Suffice to say that he kisses very well. . . ." Marsha broke off and blushed brightly. "And I do hope to see him again, very soon."

"Thank you," Amy said with dignity. "That's all I wanted to know."

"Satisfied, nosy?" Rick teased. Amy nodded unrepentantly.

The waitress brought their meal and they served themselves egg rolls, rice, egg foo young, chicken lo mein, and moo goo gai pan. Marsha splashed everything with soy sauce and handed the bottle to Rick. "Go easy on the sauce, Amy," she cautioned. "It's full of salt." Amy made a face at Marsha but skipped the sauce.

"Heard from Mother this week?" Amy asked as she took a bite of her egg roll.

"No, but I did hear from Jerry this morning," Marsha replied as she sampled the egg foo young.

"And what's he up to?" Amy asked warily.

"The usual," Marsha said dryly. "He's got a new job, the one that's going to make him rich and famous in three weeks."

"Where is he now?" Rick asked as he forked up some rice. Although he and Amy had married after Marsha's divorce, he had heard more than one conversation about Marsha's ex.

"Florida," Marsha said as she drank a little of the delicious hot tea. "He's got a job as a bartender."

"Well, who knows, this time he might make it," Rick said thoughtfully. Marsha was conscious of a charitable streak in Rick that was notably lacking in herself and Amy.

"I wouldn't put money on it, Rick," Amy said. "Speaking of money, has he ever repaid you for his lawyer's fee?"

Marsha shook her head. "And you know as well as I do that I'll never see that money," she replied frankly.

Amy rolled her eyes in exasperation. "You never should have loaned it to him, you know," she admonished Marsha gently.

Marsha bridled at the criticism. "Maybe it was worth it to get rid of him," she said shortly.

"Sorry," Amy muttered. Marsha sat in silence, regretting she had snapped at Amy that way. Her sister was too kind to come out and say it, but Marsha had shown very poor judgment when she had loaned Jerry the money. In fact, she had shown very poor judgment in having anything to do with Jerry. Rick changed the subject and they finished their meal, then drove back to the Planned Parenthood office where Marsha taught her classes.

Marsha unlocked the outer door of the building and opened the door of the large, comfortable room where she taught her classes. Amy followed her in, bringing the prescribed two pillows, and Rick followed her, a camera case in his hand. He had offered to take a series of pictures during the course of the sessions for Marsha, and she suspected it was as much for his own pleasure as to help her out. Amy plunked down the pillows and sat down on one. Rick sat down beside her and opened his camera case, popped out a camera, and took a picture of

46

Amy sitting cross-legged on the floor. "You look like a grape on a toothpick," he commented idly.

Marsha laughed as Amy stuck out her tongue at him. "It's your grape, buddy," Amy snapped back teasingly. "And your toothpick."

The other six couples that were signed up for the class began to drift in. The expectant parents chatted with one another as Marsha hauled out her charts and her diagrams. Ninety percent of a successful delivery was education, and Marsha prepared her prospective parents thoroughly for what they should expect during the last few weeks of pregnancy and after the birth as well as for the labor and delivery itself. Mrs. Gilbert had telephoned and said that a new couple had called and would be coming to the classes tonight, and Marsha wondered who would be signing up at this late date. She was setting up the last of her charts when a familiar voice spoke behind her. "Excuse me. Are you the nurse who will be teaching the course?"

Marsha turned on her knees and stared up in shock, the color rushing to her face and leaving it just as quickly. Ward stood towering over her, and beside him stood a very pretty, very pregnant young woman about her own age. Legs trembling with stunned reaction, she stood up shakily and nodded her head. "Actually, I'm the midwife," she said through stiff lips, staring at the two people standing in front of her.

Maybe there's an explanation, Marsha pleaded with herself. Maybe she's the wife of a friend. Maybe he's just dropping her off. *No,* her mind screamed. *It can't be. He can't be married.* She looked up into Ward's eyes, hoping that her face didn't betray her shock.

Ward seemed surprised but not particularly disturbed to see her. "Hello, again," he said easily. "I didn't realize Katy had called your office."

47

I'll just bet you didn't, Marsha thought cynically, although one part of her mind was still hoping for an explanation. She turned to the woman and extended her hand. "I'm Marsha Walsh," she said as the woman grasped her hand firmly.

"I'm Katy Sentell," she said softly. "I hope you don't mind me signing up at this late date. You see, I just moved to town a few weeks ago and was looking for a doctor. Ward mentioned that I might want to use a midwife instead, and I liked the idea, so here I am! I have an appointment on Friday with you." She looked up and smiled at Ward with love in her eyes. He looked down at her tenderly.

"That's super," Marsha said as she fought to stay calm. I don't believe this, she said to herself. He takes me out last night until all hours, then goes home and tells his wife to call a midwife to deliver her! What on earth kind of louse is this man? She ventured another look at Katy. Although the woman was very pretty, there was a lurking sadness about her eyes. She knows, Marsha thought. She knows something isn't right. Marsha looked up at Ward and was horrified when he winked broadly at her when Katy would not see. What a bum! Marsha thought. What a real bum! She sneaked a look over at Amy, who was staring with open-mouthed astonishment at the three of them. Amy leaned over and whispered something to Rick, who shrugged his shoulders and shook his head.

Ward and Katy sat down on their pillows and Marsha sat down beside her charts. "Good evening," she said brightly, hoping her inner turmoil did not show on her face. "Since I know all of you but you don't know each other, I'd like you to go around the circle and introduce yourselves, and perhaps tell us what you do for a living." She gestured to the couple on her left, who introduced themselves as Pat and Mary Contreras and said that they

48

were both legislative aides at the capitol. Each couple introduced themselves in turn. When they came to Ward and Katy, Ward introduced them simply as Ward and Katy Sentell, although he did mention that he was with the university. As the next couple spoke, Ward caught Marsha's eye and gave her another flirtatious wink.

Damn him, he has his nerve, Marsha thought as the class continued. Every time she looked his way, he sent her a warm smile, or a little wink, or a teasing grin, all designed to remind her of the night before. Fortunately, Marsha had taught so many childbirth sessions, she could teach the first one in her sleep if need be. Her mind certainly wasn't on her teaching tonight. Mechanically, she went through the process of labor and delivery, explaining what happened at each point and carefully outlining the father's role in each step, wondering if Ward would be there to go through it with Katy or if he would be out on another date where Katy could not reach him. She explained some of what to expect at both a home and a birthing center delivery and hoped that Katy would opt for the birthing center, dreading the thought of having to go to the home that Ward and Katy lived in and deliver Katy on the bed that she and Ward shared. Marsha outlined what to bring to the birthing center or to have on hand at home and wondered if Ward cared enough to help Katy pack her things. She answered questions from all the couples, including two from Katy, ignoring the sensual smile that Ward sent her way. Damn him, how could he? How could he do it to Katy? How can he do it to me? Finally, she had covered the information that she always included in the first session. She reminded everyone that the next meeting would be next week, same time and place, and wished the class a good evening.

As the prospective parents chatted among themselves, Marsha knelt down and began gathering up her charts and diagrams, putting them into a neat pile. As a warning sensation ran down her spine and a tall shadow fell across the charts, she looked over her shoulder at Ward, then moved away and picked up the charts, trying to stand up with them in her arms. Losing her balance, she fell back on her heels. Ward reached down and grasped her hand, pulling her up slowly. In spite of her anger at him, tremors of sensual pleasure ran down at the touch of his fingers, and she jerked her arm back as though it had been stung.

If Ward noticed anything out of the ordinary about her attitude, he didn't let on. "You teach a mean class," he whispered, a wicked grin on his face.

"Thank you," Marsha said stiffly. "I'm delighted that you went home and told Katy all about it." She looked around for Katy but spotted her across the room talking to the Contrerases.

"Yes, she liked the idea," Ward said easily.

"She seemed to, didn't she?" Marsha said evenly.

"Listen, I'm sorry I didn't call you today. I was busy," Ward said.

"I'll just bet you were," Marsha said sarcastically. This time Ward couldn't help but notice her attitude.

"Look, I'm sorry I didn't get to it," he said. "I'll call you about the weekend, I promise."

"Don't bother," Marsha said caustically.

"What the . . ." Ward sputtered.

"Ward, I think we better go," Katy said as she walked up to them. Marsha looked at Katy closely, wondering if she had heard any of the exchange. The woman's face was pensive again, although she directed no hostility toward Marsha. Maybe she doesn't know about last night, Marsha thought, but she does know something isn't right.

"I enjoyed the class," Katy volunteered. Ward looked

furiously at Marsha and started to speak, but Katy laid her hand on his arm. "We really do need to go," she said softly. "You have to get up at five."

"Good night," Marsha said as they walked across the room and left by the front door. Damn you, Ward, why did you have to be a cheat? she asked herself as she let out the breath that she had been unconsciously holding. For some reason he had looked as though he were about to make a scene, but he could hardly have done that in front of Katy. Dispiritedly, Marsha picked up the charts and locked them in the closet, then left the building and climbed in the van, sitting morosely as Rick and Amy climbed in and shut the doors.

Amy turned around and looked at Marsha with wide, sad eyes. "Marsha, I didn't know," she said quietly. "In all the months we've worked together, he's never mentioned her."

"That's all right," Marsha said dejectedly, scuffing her foot on the floor of the van. "It's hardly your fault."

"Did he say anything last night about a wife?" Amy asked curiously.

"Do you think I would have gone dancing with him if I'd known?" Marsha asked bitterly. "I haven't stooped to dating married men knowingly, Amy."

"I know that," Amy said softly. She looked at Marsha with concern in her eyes. "I'm sorry, Marsha."

Rick pulled up in front of her apartment and hopped out. She got out on his side, trying not to notice the concern in his eyes. "Are you all right?" he asked worriedly.

"Sure, I'm fine, both of you," she assured them as Amy peered at her anxiously. "It was just a date. We weren't engaged or anything." She forced herself to summon a smile. " 'Night, you two," she called with false gaiety.

51

Rick got back into the van and Marsha watched them drive away with an emotion burning in her breast that she dimly recognized as jealousy. For the first time in her life, she was bitterly jealous of her older sister. Damn it, Amy, how did you catch a man as nice as Rick? What did you do right that I didn't? Angrily, Marsha reached out with her foot and kicked a rock across the parking lot, then swore out loud. "Damn, damn, damn," she said into the still night. "Why do I have to pick all the bums?"

CHAPTER THREE

Marsha stood in front of her building, staring up at the empty apartment, and sighed. She knew that if she went in and tried to go to sleep, she would instead toss and turn for most of the night, remembering the feel of Ward's treacherous body against hers, reliving the way his lips made her body sing. Damn him, anyway! On impulse, Marsha riffled through her keys and found the one that unlocked the small storage closet reserved for the tenants. Dragging out her shiny red bicycle, she locked the closet behind her and hopped on. Her mother, Amy, and Mrs. Gilbert would turn three shades of horrified if they could see her riding alone at night, but maybe if she rode awhile she could shake off the paralyzing sense of—what? Betrayal? Yes, she felt betrayed. But betrayal intimated surprise, and once the shock had worn off, Marsha had not really been too surprised tonight when Ward had walked in with his wife. So what was another loser to her? She specialized in collecting them!

Marsha pedaled out of the parking lot and onto a side street, relishing the feel of the cool air on her burning cheeks. I should have known, she told herself. If there was a man who was less than he should be, I would find him. He would be drawn to me like a magnet! A small gust of wind caught Marsha's hair and lifted it off her face. So what is it about me? she wondered. Why am I always their sucker? She knew that she was a little naive at times and had too generous a spirit, but was that any explanation for her continuous involvement with losers?

Marsha sighed and let her mind drift back some years to her first love and her first disillusionment. She had been shy and quiet in high school, not dating much and not particularly interested in boys. Although she had admired Amy for her brilliant scholastic achievements and had grown heartily sick of being compared to her brilliant older sister, she had no desire to follow in Amy's footsteps, preferring to pursue a people-oriented career. So she chose nursing, and with her superior grades and her parents' generosity she went to Baylor. She dated a variety of college boys once or twice during her two years in Waco, but she never felt the slightest attraction for them. They were fun to date, that was all. Then she had moved to Dallas to finish her training, and had met Jerry Bradshaw.

Marsha slowed her bicycle and turned onto another side street, riding by dimly lighted houses and a few that were already plunged into total darkness. Jerry, tall and good-looking, had been the first man who had ever stirred her spirit. He was a few years older than she, and she was so attracted to him that she did not stop to wonder why, at twenty-six, he was no further along in college than she was. She had fallen hard for his boyish good looks, the blond hair that shone white in the sun, and the crooked smile that turned her knees to jelly. He had charmed her thoroughly. They had dated regularly, although they had gone on a lot of picnics and other inexpensive outings, and Marsha had taken him home to meet her parents. Her mother had loved him immediately, and if her father had his doubts, he did not express them. Jerry begged her to marry him, and they were married at the end of her junior year in a small ceremony in her mother's living room.

Maybe we should have stayed on our honeymoon forever, Marsha thought sourly as she slowed for a stop sign. That was about the only good time we had. They had honeymooned in Corpus Christi and had returned to Dallas to take the summer jobs that they had lined up. Jerry had liked his. He liked it so much, in fact, that he announced at the end of August that he was not going back to school, but would continue working for the restaurant where he had been hired. It was a great future, the bosses insisted, and he really didn't need a degree to do the job. At the time Marsha had been dismayed, but there wasn't much she could do to stop Jerry. So he dropped out of SMU and went to work for the restaurant full-time.

Marsha reached up and brushed away a strand of hair that had blown in front of her face. And how long did that job last? she asked herself. Three months. That was one of the long ones, she remembered cynically. By November Jerry was tired of the routine and the discipline, so over dinner one evening he calmly announced that he had quit his job and was going to look for something better. Marsha had been horrified, but Jerry had reassured her that everything was going to be fine and that he would find something really great, just watch. And sure enough, with his charm he managed to land a management training position with a major Dallas firm early in the new year. They must have really wanted some work out of him, Marsha thought as she wheeled her bicycle around a cul-de-sac and headed back down the street. He lasted there for only two weeks.

Unfortunately, Jerry's pattern was set, and there was little that Marsha or anyone else could do to change it. While Marsha finished her training and worked part-time in the hospital, Jerry tried two more jobs that spring, quickly finding fault with each situation and quitting. They had survived on her part-time salary and help from her parents until she received her degree and was offered a very good job in one of the best hospitals in Dallas. Although her professional life thrived, her marriage continued to go downhill. Jerry would sporadically hunt for a job, but if he found one, he wouldn't stay at it for more than a month or two, leaving it when he found that it involved a certain amount of work. Most of the time he would sit around the apartment and daydream, regaling Marsha every evening when she would drag her exhausted self in the door with his wild schemes for making it big. At first Marsha listened to him, hoping to find a glimmer, a thread of hope that maybe Jerry would turn out to be something after all, but as the months wore on her hope died as did her love for him. Jerry was a hopeless drifter, a dreamer, and that was all there was to it. Marsha realized that many women could have put up with Jerry and his dreams, willing to love him for his looks and his charm and ignore the rest, but Marsha simply was not made that way. She let the marriage go on for months longer than it should have, knowing it had to come to an end but not quite sure how or when to end it.

Marsha sighed and slowed her bicycle, cautiously crossing a busy, well-lighted intersection before entering another neighborhood. Close to the campus, the old houses on this block had mostly been converted into apartments and were rented by students at U.T. The lights were brighter coming out of the students' apartments, and Marsha could see occasional activity in the windows and at the doors. I bet this is a real party row on weekends, she thought briefly before her thoughts returned to Jerry and her failed marriage. The issue of their marriage had come to a head in a most unexpected way.

Marsha had done well at nursing but had found that she really didn't like the hospital routine all that much. The patients were cranky, the doctors were bossy, and the supervisors critical, and she began to feel stifled doing the same thing every day. Then one afternoon a woman from a nurse-midwifery school in Mississippi came to speak to the nurses at her hospital. Marsha heard her speak and found herself quite interested in the specialty. She was even more pleased when she found that she could get her training in Dallas, so she called the Dallas school and asked for an application. She went home that night and told Jerry very enthusiastically about her plans, explaining very carefully that it would mean a year off from work but saying that he could get a job and that they would survive. Jerry seemed to take it well, but a week later Marsha came in and found his bags packed and Jerry walking out the door. He gave her the telephone number of a mutual acquaintance, another nurse at the hospital, and said that Marsha could call him there when she had arranged a divorce.

For a few days Marsha had been shocked, but then sheer relief had taken over and she had quickly filed for a divorce, promising herself that once she was rid of Jerry she would run just as far from him and all the other Jerrys in the world as she could. She had made a mistake in him, but everyone made mistakes, didn't they? So once her divorce was final she had signed up for the nurse-midwife training that was offered in Dallas, and while waiting the four months for the next classes to begin, she had begun dating. Most of her dates were like those she had had in Waco—the men were nice, but they did not really appeal to her in any special way. And then, in the Laundromat, she met Jack. A bitter smile touched Marsha's mouth as she remembered Jack.

He was a car dealer, he said, and from the look of the

57

diamond ring on his right hand and the expensive clothes he was carelessly shoving into the washer he must have been a good one. They chatted while their clothes washed and Marsha impulsively accepted a date with him for the following evening, on which he had taken her to one of the nicest restaurants in Dallas, dropping seventy-five dollars on dinner as though it were nothing. Marsha, who had scrimped so during her two years with Jerry, had thought she was in heaven. In the weeks that followed, Jack regularly treated Marsha to nights out on the town, spending money on her as fast as he could. On occasion he entertained her at his elegant Highland Park apartment, which he had furnished with expensive antiques in the finest of taste. Enjoying herself thoroughly after living so frugally, Marsha did not stop to think that Jack's style of life went well beyond that of a car dealer, even a good one. She just enjoyed herself and was beginning to fall for Jack in the same way that she had fallen for Jerry, when she was presented with a rather rude shock about Jack.

I wonder how long it would have gone on if we hadn't seen that silly advertisement? Marsha asked herself as she turned her bicycle around and headed back toward her apartment, a grim smile on her lips. Although at the time she had been crushed, in retrospect the entire incident was almost funny. Since Marsha was on the night shift, she was able to date Jack only two nights of the week, and trusting Marsha never gave a thought to what Jack did on the other nights, since he called her frequently at the hospital during her shift to tell her hello. She naively assumed that he was working or at home on those evenings. And she would probably have gone on thinking that if she and three of the other nurses, bored on a slow night, hadn't read the want ads and found an ad for a discreet ladies' "escort" service and a post office box number. Giggling, the four nurses had written a letter

58

inquiring about the service, and a week later they had received a letter in the mail intimating that the escorts were available for much more than providing an escort and conversation, which was about what the nurses had expected. What Marsha had not expected was to find Jack's picture in the stack of potential escorts.

Now, looking back on the confrontation scene, Marsha could almost laugh. She had been horrified, shocked, amazed, that Jack could even do such a thing. Jack, on the other hand, simply could not understand Marsha's reaction. So what? he said. It was just a part-time job. It had nothing to do with his feelings for her. And besides, the money was very good. When Marsha realized that Jack simply could see nothing wrong with what he was doing, she had broken off the relationship with him and, sick of Dallas, she had applied to the midwifery school in Mississippi and moved there to take her training. She had dated very little in Mississippi and even less often in Austin, in part because her work was so demanding and in part because she was sure that she would automatically choose another loser.

Which you did the minute you let your guard down, she told herself cynically as she wheeled back across the busy intersection. You went out and found yourself a married cheat this time. All you can find is losers, Marsha, so why don't you just quit trying? You did it again last night. You picked out the stinker. Marsha sighed, knowing that there had to be nice men out there. Her father was wonderful, and Rick was everything that a woman could hope for in a man. But that kind of man simply did not come her way.

Marsha pedaled into the parking lot of her apartment and locked her bicycle in the storeroom. Running up the stairs, she unlocked her apartment and went inside, stripping off her jeans and shirt and standing under the

59

shower while the cool water poured over her weary body. Was there some fault in her that attracted the wrong kind of man? she wondered as she squirted shampoo in her hair. Do I wear a big sign that says SUCKER HERE? She let the spray rinse the soap out of her hair and soaped her body thoroughly, rinsing it under the shower, then stepped out and pulled on her baby-doll pajamas. Going to the kitchen, she poured herself a glass of milk and carried it to the couch, wincing when she realized that Amy had seen everything tonight—her excitement about Ward and her embarrassing humiliation when he had come in with his wife. Although she did not experience a return of the bitter jealousy she had felt in the parking lot this evening, she admitted to herself that she envied Amy, not for her brilliant career, but for the sound judgment that she always seemed to exhibit. Amy always has her act together, Marsha thought wistfully. She not only is managing a great career, but her marriage is wonderful and her husband is a doll. How do you do it, Amy? How did you pick a winner? How does any woman pick a winner? Damn it, I wish I knew. I'm tired of Amy watching me screw up and then having her worry about me. I wish I could do something right for a change!

Marsha rinsed her glass at the sink and wandered into the bedroom. I just can't trust my judgment about men, she thought as she pulled the covers up. Jerry, Jack, Ward—they're all alike. Bums, every one of them. Thoroughly disgusted with herself, Marsha pulled the covers over her head and cried herself to sleep.

Marsha ran up the stairs and fumbled with her key as the telephone in her apartment pealed out through the windows. Awkwardly, she shifted her bag of groceries to her other arm and unlocked and threw open the door, hurrying toward the telephone, since she had three pa-

60

tients who were due to deliver at any time and she had neglected to take her beeper with her to the grocery store at the end of the block. Panting a little, she picked up the receiver and said, "Marsha Walsh."

"Hello there, my beautiful midwife. Did I catch you at a bad time?"

Marsha's hand froze in the act of setting down her groceries and her voice stuck in her throat. Ward! He had said that he would call, although after he had appeared at her class with his wife, she really hadn't thought he would have the nerve. Treacherous memories of his mouth on hers tormented her as she gripped the receiver in a stranglehold.

"Marsha? Are you there?" Ward demanded.

"Yes, I'm here," she said finally. What could she say to him? Get lost? You have your nerve? You bastard? Marsha started to give him a piece of her mind, then decided that a sophisticated brush-off might be more appropriate, since he and Katy would be attending her class, and Amy had to work with him every day. "So how have you been?" she asked in her best bored voice.

"Fine, just fine," Ward said warmly, his sensual aura radiating out over the telephone. Damn it, did a cheat have a right to be so appealing? "I did say I'd call you about this weekend. Would you like to go out? How about Saturday?"

And what do you plan to do with poor Katy on Saturday? Marsha wondered to herself. "No, I don't think so, Ward," she said lightly. "Something's come up, and I'm afraid I'm going to be rather busy." In spite of her disgust with him, she found it hard to mouth the words. In spite of what she knew about him, one part of her wanted to go.

"Well, how about Friday then?" Ward asked pleasantly.

Damn you, you're not going to make this easy, are you? Marsha thought in despair. "No, Ward, I don't really think so," she said coolly.

"Very well. I'll see you Wednesday night," he said curtly. "Good night." Marsha shivered as she hung up the telephone. Ward's voice had gone hard and cold. He was angry, she could tell, and he had also sounded hurt. But then so was she, she reminded herself as she carried her bag of groceries to the kitchen. Ward was trying to cheat on his wife with her, and he didn't even have the finesse to try to hide the fact that he was married. So why should she care if his feelings were hurt? He certainly hadn't cared if he hurt hers!

Marsha eased out the tiny head and immediately suctioned the small nose with a syringe. "One more push, Judy," she said as the young teacher pushed with all her strength. The wet, slippery baby slid from its mother and immediately set up a lusty cry. "It's a girl, Judy!" Marsha crowed as she laid the baby on her mother's chest. Immediately soothed by Judy's heartbeat, the tiny infant squawked one more time and stuck her thumb in her mouth, looking around the room with eyes that wouldn't quite focus. Deftly Marsha took care of Judy while the new mother touched her baby with gentle, exploring fingers. Sam, Judy's husband, leaned over and fondled his daughter's foot with his huge hand.

"Well, what do you two think of her?" Marsha asked as she picked up the tiny girl and laid her on the examining table to one side of the birthing bed, quickly going over the baby with gentle, experienced fingers.

"Gosh, she's just beautiful, Marsha," Sam said as he looked at his baby in awe.

"No, she's not, she looks like a squashed prune," Judy

62

teased, her bright smile revealing her delight with her new daughter.

"Well, even if she does look a bit manhandled now, you just give her a few days!" Marsha said with mock indignation. "This little lady's going to be wowing the fellas right and left. By the way," she said as she pinned on a diaper and wrapped the baby in a soft blanket. "What's her name?"

"Jean."

"Natalie," the young parents said the two names in unison. They looked at each other in surprise, then grinned sheepishly. "I thought you had given up that silly name," Sam said to Judy.

The grin faded from Judy's face, to be replaced by a look that was almost belligerent. "We are *not* calling her Jean after your mother," Judy replied firmly.

"But you promised . . ." Sam began as Judy's face turned mutinous.

"Natalie Jean, let's get you acquainted with your mother," Marsha broke in hurriedly before the young parents could escalate the argument any further. She thrust the baby in Judy's arms as the new mother was about to hurl invectives at her husband, and her stream of abuse turned into a coo of delight as the tiny girl reached out with a tiny flailing fist. Marsha put her things away and prepared to leave the new parents. "Now, Judy, Sam, as far as I'm concerned, you can leave here as soon as you feel up to it, but since it's so late, you might want to sleep a few hours and go home in the morning. Now, remember that I'll be out in three days to check you, Judy, and Natalie Jean, too, but you need to be looking for a regular pediatrician to take her on. All right?"

"Sure thing," Judy said as she cuddled her baby. "By the way, Natalie Jean doesn't sound half bad."

"Yeah, I like it too," Sam said as he bent over and gave his wife an awkward kiss.

"See you in three days, then," Marsha said warmly as she walked out of the birthing room and through the cheerfully decorated birthing center. Although Marsha did like to do home births, she also liked the friendly, homey atmosphere of the birthing center, and she appreciated the fact that, in case of emergency, the birthing center was only minutes away from the hospital. Glancing at her watch, she gasped at the time and quickened her pace to the door. She was supposed to be teaching her childbirth class right now. Banging the door behind her, she raced to her car and slammed it in gear, pulling out of the parking lot and driving down the street just as fast as she could get away with. She made it to the Planned Parenthood offices in record time, parking under a huge cottonwood tree and taking a deep breath before she got out of the car. Tonight she would have to face Ward again, and her heart pounded in apprehension at the thought of seeing him.

He had not called her since she had brushed him off last week, yet he had never been far from her thoughts. Marsha was horrifyingly aware that for the first time in her life she could understand women who knowingly carried on with married men. Although she had no intention of ever going out with him again, she simply could not forget the way his mouth had tantalized hers and the way she had responded to his sensual touch. Damn, why did he have to be out of reach? Marsha wailed to herself as she stepped out of the car and walked to the offices. Ward, you are a rat of the highest order, Marsha thought disgustedly, but I'm still attracted to you.

Taking a deep breath, Marsha strode into the teaching room and smiled brightly at her pupils, willing herself not to seek out Ward's face. As she greeted the class she caught Amy's eye and smiled at her worried-looking sister, then she sat down on the floor with the class. "I'm sorry I'm late," she apologized as her class waited expectantly. "There's a new cry going out in Austin tonight."

The class laughed obligingly and Marsha allowed herself to glance around the room. Katy Sentell, who had come in for an exam on Friday, had joined in the laughter, but Ward was staring at her coldly. So you're going to pout, she thought as she let her glance travel to the next couple. So pout! See if I care.

"Tonight we're going to discuss the specific signs of oncoming labor," Marsha explained to the class. "And then we'll go over some muscle-relaxation techniques that will help you through the early stages of labor." She pointed to one of her charts and explained just what the process of labor amounted to, then showed the class diagrams of the changes the women could look for in their bodies that would hint that the big event may not be far off. The couples were interested and asked many good questions. Marsha gratefully immersed herself in her teaching and determinedly ignored the cold, unfriendly looks that Ward was continually directing her way. Step by step she and the class discussed each and every sign that nature gave to alert the potential mothers that labor was imminent, and she went over the physical sensations that they could expect during this stage. Reassuringly, she explained to Pat Contreras that there was usually plenty of time to go home and get a prepacked bag if Mary went into labor at the capitol, but she suggested that all the husbands, particularly Rick, since he lived out of town, not venture too far from a telephone as the time became close. And where will you be, Ward? she wondered as Katy raised her hand to ask a question. Will you be at home with her, or will you be out with someone else as gullible as I was? she thought bitterly.

"I think it would be nice if we stopped for a break," Marsha said as the question-and-answer session wound down. "There's a Coke machine in the corridor if you want a drink, but, please, moms, stick to the ones without caffeine!" Tiredly Marsha pushed herself off the floor and rubbed her aching back. Out of the corner of her eye, she could see Ward follow Katy in the direction of the Coke machine. Once they had left the room, Amy got up as quickly as she could from the floor and made a beeline for Marsha.

"So what gives?" Amy asked in a whisper. "Did he call you?"

"He sure did," Marsha said dryly. "Actually got miffed because I said I was busy."

"Busy? Why didn't you just come out and tell him the truth?" Amy demanded indignantly. "I certainly would have!"

"Because he happens to work with my sister, and I don't want to make things uncomfortable for her at her place of employment," Marsha reminded her dryly.

"Well, thanks," Amy said. "But you don't have to worry about me, Marsha. In fact, I may just say something to him myself!"

"Oh, it wouldn't do any good," Marsha replied tiredly. "That kind are all alike. Just let it go, Amy. Don't spoil your professional relationship with the man." She rubbed her tired neck and reached into her pocket for change. Yes, she had enough for a soft drink, so she left Amy talking with a young attorney and her husband and headed for the Coke machine. She glanced around, but the corridor was deserted and Ward was nowhere to be seen, so she relaxed a little and pulled out sixty-five cents for a Coke.

As she bent down to pick up her can, the door of the men's rest room flew open and Ward strode through, his grin fading to a scowl as he spotted Marsha at the machine. "So how have you been?" he asked curtly.

"Fine, just fine," Marsha replied levelly, hoping that the quavering in her knees didn't show in her voice. Seeing Ward this close, she was almost overwhelmed by his devastating masculinity and it was all she could do not to throw her principles out the window. She popped the top off of her can and headed for the teaching room.

A firm hand on her arm stopped her in mid-stride. She looked up, startled, as Ward's angry gaze burned down on her. "So you're fine and I'm fine, but you won't see me and you brush me off with a lame excuse about being busy. I'd like to know what the hell's going on."

Marsha swallowed back the angry retort that sprang to her lips. "I said I was busy and I was," she replied frankly. In fact, she had been busy, spending most of both Friday night and Saturday night delivering babies.

"So what about this weekend?" Ward demanded. "Are you free?"

"No, I'm not," Marsha said coolly, trying in vain to loosen her arm from Ward's stranglehold yet despising herself for not really wanting the contact to end. Damn, it wasn't fair, this sensual power he held over her.

"And just why aren't you free?" Ward demanded imperiously. "You liked me well enough the other night. Or do you kiss everybody like that?"

Marsha paled at his cruel taunt. "I didn't know I was poaching the other night," she said softly. "Let me go, Ward, before Katy sees you." Abruptly Ward let go of her arm and on shaking legs she walked back into the teaching room, gagging down a few swallows of her now unappetizing soft drink. As she set aside the drink, she saw Ward walk back in the room with Katy, his arm settled gently around Katy's waist. In spite of herself,

67

Marsha wished for just a moment that it was her waist that Ward was so casually holding.

I wonder what the hell went wrong, Ward thought as he lay on the carpeted floor, trying and failing miserably to obey Marsha's quietly voiced instructions to relax. He dutifully contracted the muscles in his arm and then, on Marsha's command, he let his arm relax onto the floor, limp. Beside him Katy tightened and relaxed her arms obediently, totally oblivious to the anger that was eating him alive. Thank goodness Katy can't tell how upset I am, Ward thought as he glanced over at the tired woman. She has enough to cope with right now. Tightening the muscles of his right leg as Marsha was instructing, he relived that devastating kiss that he and Marsha had shared in her front seat, and desire curled in his loins as it had every time he had thought about her. Damn, she liked me the other night, I know she did, Ward thought angrily as Marsha soothingly instructed the class to relax their entire bodies. How the hell am I supposed to relax, woman, he thought bitterly, when I want you so much I can taste it and you won't even give me the time of day? He glanced over at Amy Patterson, dutifully relaxing into the carpet, and scowled to himself. And something's been eating her all week, too, he thought. Amy had always been lovely to him before, but this week she had been as cold as ice, barely speaking except when she had to. So what's with the two of them? he wondered as Marsha informed the class that they could sit up.

Ward sat up and reached for Katy, pulling her up to a sitting position and planting a tender kiss on her forehead. He looked across the room and was astonished to see an expression of pain, almost anguish, pass across Marsha's face before she could stop it. Damn you, woman, why do you have me tied up in knots like this?

he wondered sourly even as he longed to take her into his arms and kiss away whatever her hurt was. As she glanced around the room, her gaze fell on him and Katy and hardened perceptibly before it passed on to the next couple.

Damn it, that does it, Ward thought as Marsha bade the class good-night. I'm going to have it out with her, and I'm going to do it tonight. I'm going to find out what the hell's eating both sisters. Determinedly, he pushed himself up off the floor and started toward Marsha, anger in his eyes, when he heard a soft voice behind him. "Ward, are you all right?" Katy asked uncertainly.

"Of course, Katy," he replied as he turned around and helped her up. He looked down at her and made himself quell his determination. No, it wouldn't do to make a scene in front of Katy, but he would have it out with Marsha, and he would do it soon. "Are you tired, hon?" he asked as he reached down and picked up the pillows.

"Sure am, Ward," she replied softly.

"Then let's go home," he said, smiling at Katy fondly.

Marsha popped out her TV dinner and sampled a bite of the mashed potatoes from the middle of the serving. Yes, they were hot—dinner was served! Eagerly she placed the dinner in the middle of a tray and wandered out into the living room, putting the tray on the coffee table and returning to the kitchen for utensils and a glass of iced tea. She flipped through the channels and found an old Dean Martin movie, but turned the television to another channel halfway through supper when she realized that the movie was an old comedy about a romantic triangle. A rehash of the last city council meeting did not appeal to her either, so she turned off the set and ate her meal in silence, wondering in spite of herself about Ward. What was he doing tonight? Was he out, or was he home with his wife? Why had he approached her last night when she had shown him so clearly that she did not want to see him again? Was his ego that colossal?

Damn it, Marsha, you can do better than that, she thought in disgust as she finished her dinner and threw the plate in the garbage. You don't have to spend the evening pining over that one! She peeked out the back window and noted that she still had the better part of an hour of daylight, and a quick spin on her bicycle would be just the thing to soothe her spirits. Humming softly, she changed her shoes and grabbed up her keys and threw open the door, finding herself staring with astonishment up into Ward's hard face, his finger hovering near the doorbell.

Oh, no, what is he doing here? Marsha asked herself in despair. Couldn't he ever take no for an answer? Gritting her teeth, she looked up at him coldly. "Did you want something?" she asked frostily.

"Yes, I did," Ward replied levelly, the light of battle in his eyes. "May I please come in?"

CHAPTER FOUR

Marsha looked up at Ward with dismay. From the expression on his face, he had every intention of coming in whether or not she invited him. Damn you, man, she thought, why do you have to keep coming around me? Even though he was angry, Ward radiated a sensual appeal to which Marsha could feel herself succumbing. Deliberately bringing Katy's sad face to mind, she ignored the clamor of her senses and hardened herself to his appeal. "By all means, come inside," she said coldly, stepping back so that Ward could enter her small apartment. "How did you get my address?"

Ward stepped into the small apartment and pulled the door shut behind him. "From a Mrs. Gilbert at your office," he said as Marsha gestured to the couch. He sat down, stretching his long legs out in front of him so that Marsha had to step across them to reach the chair. "I told her that Katy and I needed to make up a childbirth lesson and that you said we could come here to do it."

"Wonderful," Marsha replied wryly. "You lie to her as well as you do to the rest of us."

Ward's eyes narrowed at the jab but he let the remark go. "I didn't come here tonight to try to ask you out again," he said rather cruelly, causing Marsha's stomach to twist a little in pain even though she realized that she now had him out of her hair.

"So why did you come around then?" Marsha asked nonchalantly.

"Because whatever you told Amy about me has changed her attitude toward me entirely, and it's damned uncomfortable working with an iceberg," Ward replied. "We used to work together just fine, but now she's extremely cold and uncooperative. And I value our working relationship a whole hell of a lot," he continued heatedly. "I don't know what you said to her, but whatever it is, I'd like to know so that maybe I can salvage what was once an excellent professional relationship. Amy can be a pain when she wants to be."

Good for Amy, Marsha thought. "Actually, I didn't say a word to her," she replied honestly. "She saw the same thing I did and felt as I do about it."

"And just what do you two sanctimonious little prigs think you saw?" Ward demanded.

Marsha jumped off the chair and faced Ward on the couch, her hands on her hips. "Yes, I guess to you Amy and I do seem like a couple of sanctimonious prigs, don't we? We try to live decent, honest lives, but I guess you can't understand that, can you? A two-timing lecher like you! Out with me, trying to cheat on a pregnant wife! Bastards like you ought to be shot! And then you have the nerve to call Amy and me a couple of sanctimonious prigs because we're horrified. You do have your nerve, buster."

Ward's face would have done an Oscar winner proud. He stared at Marsha with complete astonishment. "Wife? What on earth are you talking about? I'm not cheating on my pregnant wife. I'm not even married anymore!"

"My God, you wouldn't even marry her? What kind of a rat are you?" Marsha asked in astonishment. "Good grief, Ward, every child deserves to be born legitimate.

And besides," she added angrily, "the poor little thing obviously adores you."

"Oh, I get it," Ward said slowly, his bewilderment turning to amusement. "Katy. You're mad about Katy."

"You're damn right I'm mad about Katy," Marsha stormed. "She deserves better than she's getting on this deal."

"You're right, she does," Ward said as an expression of bitterness crossed his face. "And if I could find the bastard who left her this way, I would smash his face in."

Marsha sucked in a tiny breath quickly. Could Katy have done a thing like that? "You mean it's not even yours?" she asked in genuine horror.

"Not quite," Ward replied. "Katy's my sister."

"Your sister," Marsha replied faintly. "Your *sister?*" she squeaked. "Katy is your *sister?* Oh, good night!" Marsha ran to the telephone and dialed Amy's number.

A sleepy sounding Rick answered. "Huh?" he said.

"Rick, let me talk to Amy," Marsha demanded.

"She's still down at the lab," he replied. "Can I take a message?"

"Tell her Katy's his sister."

The telephone was silent for a moment, then Rick burst into huge guffaws of laughter. "His sister? You mean Amy's been ranting and raving for the last two weeks, and she's his sister? That's priceless!" Too overcome to continue talking, Rick continued to laugh over the telephone.

"I'm glad you think it's so damned funny," Marsha snapped.

"Oh, I'm going to love the look on Amy's face when I tell her this one," Rick chortled.

"Good-bye, Richard," Marsha said, her cheeks stained red with embarrassment as she hung up the telephone. "I

73

had to let her know," Marsha said quietly as she sat back down in her chair.

"I gather your brother-in-law thought the whole thing hilarious," Ward suggested. "I could hear him laughing all the way over here."

"He wasn't laughing the night you walked in there with her," Marsha replied sharply. Then her face sobered with contrition. "Look, Ward, I'm—"

"Don't even try to apologize," Ward said as he shook his head. "The evidence was certainly condemning enough to warrant the conclusions you all drew," he admitted, his eyes starting to dance. "And when you think about it, it is funny. Imagine thinking I would have the nerve to take you out one night and show up with my pregnant wife at the next training class! Oh, boy, you must have thought I was some kind of rat!"

"A sewer rat, to be exact," Marsha said dryly, breaking Ward's hold on his amusement. He sat on the couch and laughed, Marsha glowering at him as he slid his arms around his middle and chuckled. "I'm glad you think the whole thing is so funny," she said. "Here I've spent two weeks agonizing over the fact that I actually went out with a married man and you think it's funny!"

"And you look like a ruffled kitten," Ward teased as he reached out with his long arm and mussed Marsha's hair, then pulled her down beside him on the couch. "Well, you can scrub your conscience clean. You did not, I repeat, *did not,* go out with a married man, so I want you to promise me that you will sleep the sleep of the innocent tonight."

In spite of her indignation over the entire situation a smile dimpled Marsha's cheek. "I promise I shall crawl in that bed and sleep the sleep of a baby—no, not that," she amended. "They aren't known for sleeping at night." She inched away from Ward's hard body and turned con-

74

cerned eyes on him. "What happened to Katy?" she asked. "I really like that woman."

Ward's face hardened a little. "Katy got involved last year with a fellow graduate student at Arizona State. They were living together and Katy had really fallen for the guy. When she found out she was pregnant, he announced that he wanted no part of the responsibilities of marriage or parenthood, and up and left her. I tried to convince her to get an abortion but she wouldn't."

Marsha turned horrified eyes on him. "Of course she wouldn't," she replied. "Katy isn't like that."

"Oh, so you don't believe in them any more than Katy does," Ward replied.

Marsha shook her head. "I'm not rabidly pro-life, but I can see why Katy wants to have this baby, especially if she loved the jerk who fathered it." She stood up and put her hands in her pockets, bending her head in a musing attitude. "I wish Katy had told me all this, and not just to avoid the mixup with you and Amy. As her delivering midwife, I need to know something of the emotional climate of the pregnancy. I had assumed she was in a marriage, albeit an unhappy one."

"She's better off with me than she would have been if her boyfriend had stayed around against his will," Ward stated firmly.

"Oh, I agree," Marsha replied quickly. "But later it's going to be hard on her, trying to raise that baby by herself."

"The Sentell family will stand by her," Ward replied firmly. "We'll help her raise the child."

"That's good to know," Marsha replied.

"So how about tomorrow night? Are you free?" Ward asked.

"No, I don't think so," Marsha said, still smarting from Ward's earlier remark. He had come over here to

75

repair his working relationship with Amy, not to see Marsha, and if Rick could stop laughing long enough to tell Amy that Katy was Ward's sister, he had accomplished his goal.

"Busy?" Ward asked.

"No," Marsha replied.

"Ticked off?" Ward asked.

"You got it," Marsha said as she flopped down in her big chair. "You came over here to get things squared with Amy, and if Rick can stifle his laughter long enough to tell her who Katy is, you will have gotten what you came for."

"Would you believe that I wasn't really all that worried about Amy?" Ward asked. "Not that she hasn't been definitely subzero, but I came over here mostly to try to square things with you. Then you looked at me like I was the worm in your apple, and my pride reared its ugly head. I didn't mean that about not wanting to go out with you again, Marsha. I want to. I want to a lot."

Marsha stared at Ward, surprised that he would come out and admit that his pride had made him say what he had. "Well, all right," she agreed, her heart becoming amazingly light. Ward was not married. She was free to see him! The world suddenly became a much more exciting place. "Yes, I definitely would like to go out with you," she declared. "What time and how should I dress?"

"Seven thirty, and wear a dress?" Ward asked. "We can go downtown to one of the fancy restaurants."

Marsha nodded eagerly, thinking of the delicious dinner she could expect and the delightful company she would be sharing it with. She smiled up at Ward, and the breath caught in his throat as that dazzling smile made her sparkle. She's really something, he thought as his own smile widened in return.

Ward unfolded his lanky frame from the couch and

76

ambled toward the door. "I need to be getting home to Katy," he explained. "Come on over here and lock the door behind me."

Instead, Marsha followed him out the door and locked it behind her. "I was just going for a ride when you came," she explained as she skipped down the stairs and unlocked the door to the storage closet.

"What are you doing?" Ward demanded.

"Getting out my bicycle," Marsha explained patiently. "I'm going for a spin."

"At nine o'clock at night? Marsha, it's dark!"

"So?" she asked calmly. "I ride all the time in the dark."

"But—but something might happen to you!" he protested.

"Don't be silly," Marsha replied. Now, why does everybody react like this? she wondered. It's my own neighborhood.

"But . . . no, never mind," Ward replied, shaking his head in amazement. The tiny little woman intended to ride her bicycle alone in the dark and seemed totally unaware of the danger she was putting herself in. As much as he wanted to, it wasn't his place to try to stop her. "Will you promise me that you will ride only along well-lighted streets?" he asked anxiously.

"Of course," she replied, her face softening at the concern she found in his.

As she straddled the bicycle, Ward bent down and planted a swift kiss on her nose and a more lingering one on her lips, tasting her sweetness once again and leaving Marsha with a craving for more of his kisses. " 'Night, sweet one," he said softly.

"See you tomorrow, Ward," Marsha said as she found the right pedal with her foot and lithely pushed off from the sidewalk. His sister! she thought as she pedaled out of

77

the driveway and into the street, narrowly missing a parked car and causing Ward to wince at her retreating form. Now, doesn't that beat all!

Marsha swore softly as the telephone rang. Damn, I hope nobody's in labor tonight! she thought as she grabbed a towel and rushed out of the shower. Ward was due to pick her up in twenty minutes and she had walked in the door seven minutes ago, having just delivered a six-pound girl in a home birth. She had performed her post-partum duties with her usual calm skill, giving vent to her hurry only once she was out of the house by breaking every speed law in Austin on the way home. Now, if this was another one . . . "Hello!" she said with none of her usual friendliness into the telephone.

"My, my, aren't we in a cheerful mood?" Amy teased over the wire. "I just wanted you to know that I tried to apologize to Ward this morning but he wouldn't let me, since, he said, it wasn't our faults that we didn't know. And I was so nasty to him! Honestly, I feel like a heel! And then Rick's been laughing at me for the last twenty-three hours! So what put you in such a lovely mood?"

"The fact that I'm standing here, dripping wet in a towel, and the object of this conversation is coming to pick me up for a swanky date in exactly eighteen minutes," Marsha replied sweetly.

"Oops! 'Bye," Amy laughed, banging down the receiver. At least Amy can take a hint, Marsha thought as she returned to the bathroom. Whipping off her towel, she stuck her head under the tap and rinsed the residue of shampoo out of her hair, then toweled it dry. Picking up the blow-dryer, she spent nearly ten minutes drying her hair into a smooth pageboy that fell to her shoulders like a smooth blond fall of water. Eight minutes. She raced to the bedroom and pulled out a pair of panties and the last

78

clean bra, promising herself that she would get down to the Laundromat tomorrow if it killed her. She threw open the closet door and flipped through her dresses. Although she didn't own that many, each of them had been rather expensive and they all looked good. Finally settling on a mint wraparound of silky fabric that clung to her every curve, she fumbled into a half-slip and panty hose and was putting on the dress when the doorbell rang. She glanced at the clock. Four minutes early.

Hooking the overlapping waist of the dress together, Marsha ran in her stockinged feet to the front door and threw it open for Ward. "Sorry about this," she mumbled as she let him in. "I was going to dazzle you with my poised glamor when I answered the door, but I got held up," she explained as she turned to rush back to the bedroom.

"That's fine with me," Ward replied, gently catching her arm and whirling her back around to face him. "Now I can kiss you before you get your warpaint on."

"I don't wear that m—" Marsha began as Ward lowered his lips to hers, blocking both her speech and the thought that had gone with it. He pressed her mouth close to his, capturing her lips with his own and tasting the sweetness of her. Oh, I'd forgotten how wonderful it feels in his arms, Marsha thought, but she hadn't, not really. Every day she had remembered the touch and the taste of him, even when she had tried not to, and now her body sang with delight at the reunion. Unconsciously she moved closer to him and pressed her body next to his, thrusting her small sensitive breasts against his rock-hard chest and curling her arms around his waist.

She feels so right here, Ward thought as he felt Marsha's tiny body press unashamedly against his. He let his lips release hers, then let them roam her bare face as he sampled the delight of her soft cheeks, her tender eyelids.

Even without her makeup she was beautiful to him. Oh, Marsha, where have you been for the last thirty-four years?

Slowly Ward and Marsha moved apart, their hearts pounding and their breathing rapid. "I could stand here and do this all night, but I bet you're hungry," Ward said as Marsha ran her hand nervously down her hair.

"Not for food," Marsha teased wickedly, blushing as she did so.

"Remove temptation from me! Go get ready!" Ward ordered as Marsha beat a hasty retreat.

Once in the bathroom she stared at her face in the mirror for a second before pulling out her makeup drawer. Her cheeks flushed, her eyes bright, her lips rosy, Ward had seen to it that she would not need much in the way of artifice tonight. Still, she got out her liner and eyeshadow and painted her eyes dramatically, thickening her lashes with two coats of mascara. Deciding to let her clear skin show through, she skipped foundation but deepened the color on her cheeks and painted on a peachy lip gloss that enhanced the color of her dress. Switching off the light, she left the bathroom and found a pair of high-heeled sandals and a matching purse in her closet. She winced as she stepped into the unaccustomed high heels and shoved her wallet, keys, and beeper into her purse. Now she could make her dramatic appearance. She straightened her shoulders and swept into the living room, catching her heel on the carpet runner and stumbling across the floor.

"Not used to the shoes, huh?" Ward asked as Marsha blushed a fiery shade of red.

"So much for the grand entrance," Marsha muttered as Ward laughed out loud. Putting his arm around her shoulders, he escorted her to the door and locked her apartment behind them.

"So where are we going?" Marsha asked as Ward escorted her to a gray Toyota.

"I know of a nice place on Town Lake," Ward said as he got into the car and started the engine. "Old-style southern place."

"Oh, the one that looks like a mansion on the outside," Marsha enthused. "I've never been there."

"Me either," Ward admitted. "But everyone says that it's very good."

They laughed and chatted all the way to the restaurant, the conversation light but with an undercurrent of attraction that Marsha could not deny. Now that the misunderstanding was cleared up and she felt free to be attracted to this man, her body clamored to be closer to his, her hands to touch him and roam freely. Never a promiscuous woman, Marsha was a little surprised and shaken by the depth of her response to Ward. What is so special about him? she asked herself. What makes him so different? Just then they had to stop for a light and Ward flashed Marsha a tender smile and at that moment she knew. It wasn't just sex. It was him. She was attracted to all of him. His body, his mind, his heart. Everything.

Ward drove toward the south part of town and up the side of a hill overlooking Town Lake, a small, extremely pretty in-city lake. About halfway up he pulled into the parking lot of what looked from the outside to be a stately old southern mansion. Ward opened Marsha's door for her and she took his arm as they walked toward the canopied entrance. "Is my southern accent up-to-date?" he whispered as they mounted the steps.

"Soften the *r*'s and drop the *y'all* and you'll have it made," she suggested as Ward pushed open the heavy front door. They looked around in appreciation at the foyer of the restaurant, decorated as the hall of an antebellum mansion would have been, with a hardwood floor

81

and a spiral staircase. A headwaiter in tails and gloves checked Ward's name against a reservation list and escorted them through the large dining room to a smaller one that was off to one side. Marsha felt underdressed momentarily, then she noticed with relief that most of the diners were no more dressed up than she was.

The waiter handed them each a menu and left them alone. Marsha inspected the menu with interest, noting that many old southern dishes were interspersed with more traditional restaurant fare. She quickly decided on a baked ham dish and closed her menu.

Ward stared at the menu for a little longer than she had, then he, too, closed his. Almost immediately the waiter reappeared to take their order. Marsha opened her menu and pointed out the ham and ordered a fruit salad to go with it. Ward asked for chicken and dumplings and ordered a rosé wine as a compromise between their vastly differing dishes.

"Now I know for sure that you're a country boy," Marsha teased as the waiter disappeared. "Chicken and dumplings—very country."

"Would you believe that I never ate them while I was growing up?" Ward asked. "It took Allison to turn me on to them."

"Who's Allison?" Marsha asked.

"My ex-wife," Ward explained.

"Oh, that's right, you said something about not being married anymore," Marsha mused. "How long have you been divorced?"

"Nearly four years," Ward replied. "How about you? Have you ever tried marriage?"

Marsha nodded. "I was married four years ago. It lasted less than two years."

The waiter brought Marsha's fruit salad and a lettuce salad for Ward. "We were married for five," he volunteered as he sampled his salad. "Allison made a dressing that was similar to this one, but I believe that hers was a little better."

"Allison liked to cook?" Marsha asked as she spooned up a bite of fruit.

"Oh, yes, she was a great cook," Ward said. "She was a fabulous homemaker, loved to cook and sew, and kept the house as clean and neat as a pin."

Good grief, thought Marsha as she reminded herself of her own aversion to cooking and cleaning. Marsha was firmly convinced that if you left the cooking and the cleaning long enough, they would go away of their own accord. "Allison didn't work, I take it?" she asked.

Ward shook his head. "No, she didn't have any interests beyond me and the house. I have to admit that I thought it was great."

"So what happened?" Marsha asked, her puzzlement showing clearly on her face.

"She traded me in for another husband and house," he admitted honestly. "In other words, she left me for another man."

"Why?" Marsha asked. She certainly would never have left a man like Ward. At least you don't think you would, she reminded herself. You don't know what her reasons were for leaving him.

"I honestly don't know for sure," Ward admitted. "Her leaving was a real surprise. Although I have to admit that he was able to buy her a bigger house and kitchen."

Marsha could detect a residue of bitterness in him even after all the years that had passed. "Are you still in love with her?" she asked hesitantly.

"Lord, no," Ward replied. "But I have to admit that it hurt like hell at first. I didn't go out on a date for six months after the divorce."

"That is hurt," Marsha admitted. The waiter collected the salad dishes and brought their dinner plates. "It sure didn't take me that long."

"I gather that you weren't devastated by the split," Ward commented as he cut a slice of chicken and popped it into his mouth.

"No, I wasn't devastated by the split," she admitted. "I was relieved when he left." She cut off a bite of ham and sampled it, rolling her eyes in delight at the tender, smoky flavor.

"Was it a bad marriage from the start?" Ward asked.

"Your perception of the obvious is outstanding," Marsha replied dryly. "No, I take that back. The honeymoon was great."

Ward laughed, then he sobered. "He wasn't cruel to you, was he?"

"No, Jerry isn't made like that. I think you could say that Jerry suffers from a terminal case of the get-rich-quicks-without-working-for-it. He never stayed on a job once he found out how much work was involved in holding it. He's still drifting around, finding one 'great opportunity' after another. He was a good-looking charmer, but I just couldn't put up with that."

"Maybe you'll have better luck next time," Ward suggested gently.

With my track record for attracting losers? Marsha asked herself. Sure. She opened her mouth to tell Ward about Jack and her own fears, but shut it over a bite of ham instead. No, she wasn't about to admit that she had doubts about the kind of man who was attracted to her and to whom she was attracted. Ward might find her fears silly, or he might be insulted. After all, he was attracted to her himself, wasn't he? And wasn't she attracted to him? It would be better to say nothing about her insecurity to him.

"Was Amy back to her old self today?" Marsha asked as she sipped the delicious wine that the waiter had poured for her.

"Yes, she tried to apologize, but it wasn't necessary. She was so indignant all week. When I think back on it, it's so funny! She was just like a bristling little mama hen."

"I'm not sure whether she was more indignant on my behalf or on Katy's," Marsha admitted.

"Well, I'm glad she's speaking again. Maybe we can get something done on this paper now," Ward admitted. "We've got the collections made and a lot of the laboratory analysis done, but we have to finish that and do the actual writing of the paper by the end of July or the middle of August. Our grant runs out then."

"Don't forget Amy will be out of commission for part of June," Marsha said.

"Looking at her, it's a little hard to forget," Ward commented as Marsha laughed. "Our schedule has taken that into account. But we will be pushing to finish so that we can go back to our regular positions in September."

"I gather you enjoyed this year of research," Marsha volunteered.

"I couldn't have enjoyed it more," Ward admitted.

"I know that Amy has enjoyed this year, but I suspect that she will be glad to get back to the classroom," Marsha said. "I know she loves teaching."

"I wish I did," Ward replied almost under his breath. Marsha started to ask him what he meant, but the waiter brought Ward the check and the moment was lost.

They walked out into the warm spring night, hand in hand, the soft breezes stirring Marsha's hair. Loath to end the evening, she and Ward walked toward the romantic spot overlooking Town Lake, twinkling lights winking across the water. Her senses spinning, she leaned into

85

Ward when he bent down and slid his arm around her and pulled her close to him, lowering his head down and capturing her lips in a kiss. Marsha arched upward, twining her thin arms around his neck and drawing his face closer to hers. They clung together, their lips locked tightly until Ward abruptly broke the embrace and glanced around. Spotting a low bench a few feet away, he picked Marsha up and carried her the few feet to the bench, standing her on the bench so that she was just a little taller than he was. "Just saving my back," he explained as he stepped closer to her and recaptured her mouth with his.

Marsha closed her eyes and let emotion wash over her. This was bliss! She wrapped her arms around Ward's neck and fondled the soft hair at his nape, moaning when he left her mouth and feathered soft warm kisses across her face and down her neck. Her senses reeling, she made no protest when he very carefully pushed aside the lapels of the wraparound dress and let his lips travel lower, finding and caressing one small breast through the lacy cup of her bra. He bathed that nipple with his lips until it swelled into a tight, ripe bud, then he moved across her chest to the other, caressing it until it, too, was hard and firm with desire. Marsha wondered how her trembling legs were holding her up, as weak with desire as they felt. Eager to explore him as he was exploring her, she ran her hands down his shirt, finding his chest hard and warm to the touch.

Slowly Ward pulled away from her, pulling the lapels of her dress together. "We're in a public place," he reminded her regretfully. "We could both be embarrassed if someone comes upon us."

"You're right," Marsha agreed reluctantly as she pulled away and straightened his collar. She looked down at her feet and grinned. "If you keep coming around, I'm going to have to buy myself a stool."

Ward laughed as he lifted her down from the bench. "I think one of those stools kids use in the bathroom would be perfect. I'm not going to let a foot difference in height stand in my way!" He took her hand and together they walked to the car, both caught up in the sensual spell they were weaving.

They drove back to Marsha's apartment in silence, kissing softly at every stoplight. Marsha's mind was spinning, and with half a mind she hoped that Ward would ask to stay the night. Normally she would never sleep with a man so soon, but if Ward asked her, she knew she would be powerless to refuse. He parked in front of her apartment and pulled her into his arms, holding her face between his hands as he bathed it in soft, light kisses, then capturing her lips in an embrace that shook Marsha to her toes. I want him to make love to me, Marsha thought nervously as Ward parted the lapels of her dress. But I shouldn't, she amended as he pushed down the lacy covering of her bra and captured one small breast with his mouth, wrapping his agile tongue around its rosy peak and tugging on it gently, sending tremors of delight down Marsha's body. Hesitantly, knowing she really shouldn't, she reached out and felt his hard chest beneath his thin shirt, feeling the slight roughness of wiry hair beneath the silken fabric. Hard and soft at the same time, she thought in wonder as her palms touched him.

"Marsha, we have to cut this out," Ward groaned as he tore his lips from her breast, pulling up her bra and pushing her dress together.

"Yes, we really do," she admitted as Ward grasped the edges of his shirt and struggled to button it with fingers that seemed to have turned to ten thumbs.

"Besides, those kids over there in the old Ford might get the right idea," Ward teased.

"Uh-oh," Marsha muttered, her face burning.

Laughing, Ward took her chin in his hand and turned her face to his. "Seriously, Marsha, you're not the kind of woman to make love lightly, and I know that, but if we don't call a halt, that's exactly what's going to happen tonight."

"I—I had figured that out already," Marsha admitted, a little disappointed but relieved at the same time. Although her body would have loved nothing better than to start a relationship with Ward, her mind and her heart knew better.

"I'll take you out again this weekend," Ward volunteered as he reached over and opened Marsha's door. "Now, get on out of this car before I change my mind. If I walk you to your door, I'll go in with you in spite of my better intentions, so I'll watch you from here."

Marsha nodded. "Good night," she said softly as she climbed out of the car and ran up the steps, Ward watching her every movement with longing on his face.

Marsha lay on her back and stared up at the ceiling, her body tired but her mind restless and spinning. It had been almost three hours since Ward had dropped her off and she had a long workday tomorrow, but she simply could not sleep. Memories of Ward's lips on hers kept intruding, stirring her into a state of reluctant arousal. But, away from the tantalizing feel of Ward's body next to hers, all of Marsha's old fears came back to haunt her. Was Ward all that he seemed? Or did he harbor hidden flaws?

Flopping over on her stomach, Marsha willed the fear to go away. He's very nice, she reminded herself. He's not married, he has a steady job, he seems all right. But that was the problem. He seemed so nice. But was he really? How could she tell if he really was or not? Jerry and Jack had seemed very nice too.

Giving up, Marsha sat up and switched on the light, picking up a medical-supply catalog and leafing through it, hoping that the boring wares displayed would put her to sleep. I really could fall for him, she thought as she threw the catalog aside a few minutes later. I really could get hurt this time. Acknowledging to herself that the attraction she felt could so easily lead to something more, she stared into space, her heart pounding. Did she dare trust her judgment about a man?

I just don't know, Marsha thought as she flopped back down in the bed. But she wasn't scared enough to back away. She would continue to see Ward, and she would just find out if he was all he seemed to be. And if she got hurt, well . . .

Marsha's telephone jangled on the nightstand. "Marsha Walsh here," she said. "About four minutes apart? Super! I'll be right there." Jumping out of bed, she threw on a pair of uniform pants and a clean white blouse, grabbing her bag and banging out of her apartment. If she had to spend a sleepless night, she might as well do it delivering a baby!

CHAPTER FIVE

"That dinner was delicious," Marsha sighed as she and Ward walked out of the elegant steak house. The air was warm in the soft June dusk and Marsha breathed in deeply and sighed.

"Yes, it was," Ward agreed. "But I don't care how good a restaurant meal is, it simply can't compare to home cooking." He took Marsha's hand and together they started toward his car.

"Hmm, I guess you're right," Marsha sighed as Ward unlocked the car door. Sliding into the car, Marsha's brow wrinkled into a frown. She and Ward had been dating for the last two months, and for the last couple of weeks he had been hinting rather strongly that he would like to have dinner at her place. And after all the money he had spent on her in the last two months, admittedly dinner at her apartment would be the least that she could offer him in return.

But the thought of cooking Ward a meal absolutely terrified Marsha. She had studiously avoided cooking when she lived at home, and made numerous excuses to avoid cooking lessons. Then she had eaten dorm food until she and Jerry had married. As an excited new bride, she had bought a cookbook and had eagerly prepared Jerry a meal every night, but he had poked such fun at them that she had quit trying after a few months and had fed him TV dinners for the remainder of her marriage. Except on the nights when she and Ward were out, that was what she still ate. And she sure couldn't warm up a TV dinner for Ward!

But Marsha realized that she had to do something. Ward had been gracious about taking her out and spending money on her, and she didn't want to hurt his feelings by refusing to extend hospitality to him. Well, maybe Amy had a simple recipe that she could cook. Taking a deep breath, she turned to Ward as he got into the car. "Would you like to have dinner at my place Thursday night?" she asked.

Ward's face split into a huge grin. "I sure would," he replied with gusto. "I haven't had a decent home-cooked meal since Allison left. Katy's not much of a cook."

"I'm not so sure that I am," Marsha muttered under her breath.

"What was that, hon?" Ward asked as he turned over the ignition.

"Nothing," Marsha said hastily. I want so to cook a good meal for him, she thought as Ward's small car sped through the streets to the movie theater where a rerun of *Gone With the Wind* was playing. An incurable romantic, Marsha dearly loved the movie and begged Ward to take her to see it. I hope I don't disappoint him when he comes over to eat.

As usual, Marsha became completely absorbed in the romantic old movie and even cried again at the end. Silently Ward handed her his handkerchief so that she could wipe the tears off her face. Then he chuckled as she handed it back to him. "What's so funny?" she demanded.

"You are," he admitted, reaching down to place a tender kiss on her lips. His eyes shining, he put his arm around Marsha as they walked to the car. "I'm really

91

looking forward to having dinner at your place. I've always enjoyed it when a woman displays her domestic talents." He hooked his arm around Marsha and pulled her to him, kissing her in full view of everyone in the parking lot.

Ward kissed her again at her door and asked what time he should arrive on Thursday. Marsha tentatively suggested seven thirty and Ward asked what kind of wine he should bring. Marsha stammered and then said that any wine would be fine. Kissing her lingeringly once again, Ward took his leave at her door as he had so often in the last two months. Marsha watched him go, the longing for him tormenting her. He had not tried to make love to her and had kept their kisses and embraces at a manageable level, and although a part of her was frustrated that he had not made love to her, the cautious side of Marsha appreciated his respect.

The next morning, in the cold light of day, Marsha berated herself mightily for inviting Ward to dinner on Thursday. Good heavens, she was no cook! How could she have agreed to something that stupid? In desperation she dialed Amy's number, but her sister had apparently already left for the university. Promising herself that she would call Amy just as soon as she got home, she showered and ate a piece of toast and left for the office.

Hal was not in the office yet, but Mrs. Gilbert was watering the plants and dusting the waiting room when Marsha arrived. "You look tired, dear," the motherly woman crooned. "Were you out delivering a baby until all hours?"

Marsha, who had slept a healthy seven hours, grimaced inwardly at the smothering concern. "No, I got plenty of sleep. These circles must be old age."

"No, it's all that hard work that you have to do. Goodness knows, you and Dr. Neimann certainly don't get the rest you need. And that sister of yours. I bet she's still working, too, isn't she? And due to have that baby any day now. You all just push yourselves too hard."

"Amy's just writing up her paper," Marsha reassured Mrs. Gilbert as she started into the offices. "That reminds me. I need to get a recipe from her."

"What kind of recipe? I certainly have a lot of good ones."

Marsha stopped in her tracks and returned to the waiting room. Mrs. Gilbert brought everyone in the office treats on a regular basis, and everything she had ever brought had been delicious. "Um, it really wouldn't matter as long as it is something simple. I'm having a, well, a friend over—"

"That nice young professor you've been seeing! Of course." Marsha's blush betrayed that Mrs. Gilbert had guessed correctly. "Well, you just go on about your business and I'll jot down one of my simple ones that you won't have any trouble with."

"Now, remember, I'm not very good in a kitchen," Marsha cautioned Mrs. Gilbert as she walked out the door.

"Don't worry, a kindergartner could do this one."

Mrs. Gilbert handed Marsha a piece of paper later in the day. "This is one of my family's favorites," she said as Marsha looked at the recipe. It was for a soufflé and consisted of no less than fifteen ingredients.

"Are you sure this is easy?" Marsha asked, thinking that she had better call Amy after all.

"I promise you. This and a salad will be all you need. He'll love it."

"Well, thanks," Marsha replied, deciding not to call Amy and promising herself that she would stop to pick up the ingredients on her way home from work. However, Pat Contreras went into labor late in the afternoon, and it was after eleven before Marsha got to the market. Exhausted, she couldn't remember whether she already had any of the ingredients or not, so she bought everything on the list, stumbling to the checkout counter in the final stages of exhaustion.

She arrived home and stuffed the perishables into the refrigerator, showered, and collapsed into bed, too tired to even pull on her nightgown.

Marsha rushed home from work on Thursday afternoon and nervously assembled all the ingredients on the counter in front of her. Easy. Mrs. Gilbert promised that it would be easy. She looked down the list of ingredients and discovered that the first ingredient was white sauce.

I haven't made a white sauce since I took home ec, Marsha thought as she pulled open cabinet after cabinet, looking for her unused cookbook. She had torn through half her cabinets when she remembered that she had given it away to the last charity book sale. Damn! She tried to call Mrs. Gilbert and then remembered that Thursday was Mrs. Gilbert's bridge day and that she would not be home until late. Knowing that Amy never cooked with sauces, Marsha knew that she was going to have to wing this one on her own. Wracking her brain, she thought that she remembered something about milk and flour, so she poured liberal amounts of each into a saucepan and heated them until the concoction started to thicken.

That hurdle out of the way, Marsha spilled three eggs into the sink before she finally got the hang of separating the white from the yolk. She followed the rest of the instructions carefully, adding a little extra salt just in case, since she hadn't put enough into the white sauce. Although the recipe didn't call for greasing the pan, she did so anyway, washing a layer of dust out of the soufflé

94

dish before she rubbed it liberally with butter and poured the mixture inside.

Setting her oven at the recommended temperature, she set the soufflé inside and quickly returned everything to the cabinets, leaving the hot kitchen gratefully and shedding her clothes in the bedroom. A quick cool shower revived her flagging energy and a soapy shampoo made her feel fresh and pretty. Aware that Ward was due to arrive in just a few minutes, she tied her damp hair behind her ears with a bow and pulled on a cheerful Mexican dress that she had purchased on her last trip to Laredo. Since Ward did not seem to care if she went light on makeup, she contented herself with just a little eye makeup and some blusher. She was just brushing on a little lip gloss when the doorbell rang.

"Hello!" she said brightly as Ward stepped across the threshold carrying a bottle of white wine.

He bent down and kissed her full on the lips, promptly removing all the lip gloss that she had just put on, then straightened and sniffed appreciatively. "What's that good smell?" he asked.

"Soufflé," Marsha said as she shut the door behind him. "It's almost ready."

"That's great," Ward replied. "I haven't had a good soufflé in years."

Not since Allison, Marsha amended to herself, irritated for even thinking it. Mrs. Gilbert promised that it would be good, she thought as she bit her lip. She said that even a kindergartner could do it. Still, she was nervous as she made a salad, Ward's long frame stretched out at her dining room table. With trembling fingers she made two tall glasses of tea and put knives and forks on the table. When the timer went off she jumped and ran for the oven, bending down to remove her masterpiece.

Mrs. Gilbert must have known some very advanced

kindergartners, Marsha thought ruefully a moment later as she looked at the fallen soufflé. Every soufflé she had ever seen was light and puffy, spilling out over the top of the pan. But this soufflé was barely two inches high in the pan, and it looked very brown and soggy. Swallowing back tears, Marsha stared at her dinner. How could she serve this to Ward?

"Is it ready yet, Marsha? I'm starved!" Ward asked eagerly as Marsha threw open the refrigerator. Was there anything else she could serve him at this late date? She jerked open the meat section and the hydrator and even the freezer, but except for the usual array of frozen dinners and a tub of ice cream, her larder was bare. She would have to serve him the soufflé.

Sorely tempted to postpone the moment by serving salad first, Marsha realized that the longer the fallen soufflé sat, the worse it would be. Gritting her teeth, she carried the pan to the table and sat it between them. "Here it is," she said brightly.

Ward looked at the soufflé and back up at her, grinning from ear to ear. "Where's the maple syrup?" he asked.

Marsha's cheeks burned as she handed him a serving spoon. "In the barnyard with the rest of the male chauvinist oinkers," she said as she picked up the glasses of iced tea and slammed them down on the table, causing tea to slosh out of the glasses.

Ward's eyes widened at the crack. "And exactly what is that supposed to mean?" he asked levelly.

"Just what I said. The maple syrup is right there with all your other outmoded ideas of how things should be." Angrily she cut a slice of the wilted soufflé and flopped it onto her plate. Then she cut one for Ward and flipped it onto his.

"For God's sake, Marsha, I didn't mean anything by it! I just thought the soufflé looked funny, that's all."

"That's all? *That's all?* I work all day long at the office and I come home and work like a dog to fix you a meal and you laugh at it! *You laugh at it!* Why are we eating here anyway? Why aren't we at your place eating your cooking?"

"Mostly because I didn't want a chaperone in the form of my little sister!" Ward shot back as he cut into the soufflé. He put a bite into his mouth and chewed it for a moment, then he swallowed and took a big sip of iced tea. He tried desperately to keep a straight face but first one chuckle escaped and then another, Marsha growing more and more furious with each guffaw that escaped. "Try it, you'll like it," he suggested.

"Never mind, I get the message," Marsha said coldly, getting up and scraping her plate into the trash. "You don't have to eat it if it's that bad."

"Aw, it's not that bad," Ward replied. "Hey, don't throw it away! Honestly, it isn't that terrible! If I can find it, I'll bring you one of Allison's old recipes."

"I don't want one of Allison's old recipes!" Marsha said as a red haze developed before her eyes. "Your ex-wife can keep her damned recipes!" She jerked Ward's plate out from in front of him just as he was aiming for it with his fork and almost got her hand stabbed with the tines.

"Marsha, you're being ridiculous, you really are," Ward said as he got up and followed her into her small kitchen. "Allison was a very good cook—all right, you don't want one of Allison's recipes," he added quickly as Marsha turned on him threateningly. "Honestly, you're overreacting, you . . ."

"Excuse me," Marsha said as she answered her ringing telephone. "Marsha Walsh here," she said, trying to calm her voice to a normal level.

"Marsha? Amy's contractions are four minutes apart," Rick said over the wire.

"Four minutes? Why didn't you call sooner?" Marsha demanded.

"We thought you might have been busy and we didn't want to disturb you until we were sure," he replied.

"Get on down to the birthing center and I'll meet you there in ten minutes," Marsha replied, hanging up the telephone and brushing past Ward. "Amy's in labor and I've got to go." She ran into the bedroom and changed to her uniform pants and shirt. "Leave the mess and I'll get it later."

"That's all right, I can clean a little of it up," Ward volunteered as Marsha dragged her bag out of the front closet. "You're leaving to deliver her now?"

"Yes, I am," Marsha muttered as she ran out the door. "That's the one thing in this life that I seem to be able to do right."

Ward watched her go, a frown of puzzlement on his face. Sure, the soufflé was a disaster, but why had she gotten so angry at his little joke? It was not a big deal—she could have warmed up a TV dinner. Shrugging, Ward loaded the dishwasher and left her apartment, locking the door behind him.

Marsha pulled up in front of the birthing center and got out of the car, her argument with Ward still bouncing around in her brain. Why did he have to make fun of her cooking? She had tried so hard to please him! Tears stinging her eyes, she willed them away, even though the feeling of inadequacy could not be controlled so easily. Why couldn't the soufflé have come out? Why couldn't she cook? It seemed like she couldn't do anything right!

Rick and Amy were waiting for her in one of the bedrooms of the birthing center, Amy clad in her own nightgown rather than white hospital issue. Rick was pacing the floor, counting aloud as Amy breathed in and out dutifully. She expelled a deep breath and smiled at Marsha. "You can quit counting now, Rick," she said wickedly. "My contraction's over."

"Oh! Sorry," Rick replied as he slowed his pace a little and sat down uncomfortably in the small armchair beside the bed.

"Amy, I want to find out how far along you are," Marsha said as Amy obediently moved her legs apart. Marsha slipped on a glove and made her examination. "Four centimeters and plus one," she said approvingly. "That's great. Now, when did you eat last?"

"Not since lunch," Amy replied. "And Rick didn't get any supper either, he was in such a hurry to get me over here," she added, taking a deep breath as another contraction started. That makes three of us, Marsha reflected as Rick coached Amy through the contraction. He's a lot more concerned than she is, Marsha thought with admiration as her sister rode the crest like a pro.

Amy continued to have contractions for the next two hours, her body slowly but surely progressing to the point where her baby could be born. After an hour she switched to the more intense breathing method, turning all her concentration inward to combat the pain of the contractions. Rick supported her with strength and confidence, his earlier jitters gone. In spite of her advanced labor, Amy managed to laugh when Rick popped out a small camera he had stuck into his pocket and snapped a few pictures of her, sweaty-browed as she rode the crest of yet another contraction.

Another hour passed and Marsha could sense that delivery was near. An examination of Amy showed that her sister had thirty minutes, maybe an hour at most, before she could start to push her baby out. "How much longer?" Rick asked as Amy took a deep breath and started blowing out sharp staccato breaths as Marsha had taught her to do.

"Not that much longer now," Marsha assured them both. "Did you hear that, Amy? It won't be that much longer."

Amy nodded and muttered under her breath as she breathed. "What was that, Amy?" Rick asked softly.

Amy muttered again. "Are you all right?" Rick asked. Amy nodded. "I couldn't hear you," he added. "Can you speak up?"

Amy nodded again. "Son . . ." Blow blow blow. "Of . . ." Blow blow blow. "A . . ." Blow blow blow. Exhale.

Oh, thank God she didn't say it, Marsha thought.

"Marsha, I want to push," Amy called out suddenly.

"Not yet, Amy. Remember, breathe out until it passes."

"Please, I think it's time," Amy replied earnestly.

"Well, let me check you," Marsha said reluctantly. "By God, you *are* ready!" She moved Amy into a more comfortable seated position. "Rick, get on some greens and a pair of gloves and get back over here. Now, Amy, when you feel the pains coming push, but not in between. You will need to rest in between. Hold on to the rails here."

"I'm ready," Rick said, standing by the bed and holding Amy's hand as she bore down for the first time.

"Look in the mirror," Marsha instructed Amy as the contraction waned.

Amy's eyes grew round. "I can see!" she said, joy lighting her tired face. "Aawp," she breathed in suddenly as another contraction came, pushing until her face became red.

"That's it, Amy," Marsha cheered as Amy pushed

100

with all her strength. "Rick, get down here. Your son or daughter is about to arrive!"

Actually, it took Amy three more good pushes before the little head was out. Quickly suctioning the nostrils, Marsha positioned Rick's hands under hers and gently guided the little shoulders and trunk out. "Lie back, Amy, your work is over now." In just a moment the entire slippery little body had emerged.

"It's a little boy!" Rick cried excitedly as Marsha laid the little body in Rick's gloved hands. He looked at the baby and then up at his wife in wonderment. "Amy, I didn't know you could do that!"

"A boy? Let me see him!" Amy demanded.

"Just a minute, Mama," Marsha teased as she cut the link that held Amy to her son. The baby let out a couple of squawks, then stared up in the general direction of his father's face and stuck his thumb into his mouth. "Here," Marsha said as she took the wiggling baby from Rick and laid him on Amy's now flat stomach. "There, now you two can bond," she teased as she took care of the rest of Amy's needs.

Rick picked up the camera and took a picture of the baby on his wife's stomach. "Five minutes old and you're turning him into a ham," Amy teased as she carefully examined the tiny naked baby that wiggled in her lap, touching his fingers and his toes almost reverently. "Can you believe it, Rick? He's really ours!"

Rick bent over and kissed Amy gently on the cheek, tears trickling down his face as he observed his wife and son. "Thank you for having him, Amy," he said as he wiped his eyes with the back of his gloved hand. Amy looked up at Rick tenderly, her eyes bright with love.

"I hate to intrude, but I need the baby for a minute," Marsha said softly as she picked up the squirming baby. She laid him on the small examining table and inspected him quickly with deft fingers, loving this tiny nephew almost immediately. "What's this little fellow's name?" she asked.

"Richard Daniel," Amy said. "But we're calling him Danny after Daddy." Their father had always gone by the nickname Danny.

"Oh, Daddy's going to be so tickled," Marsha said softly.

"But I'm afraid that square little face is pure Patterson," Rick said as he peered over Marsha's shoulder, watching her as she wiped the baby and diapered him.

Marsha looked at the baby's tiny face and laughed. "Good grief, you can see the resemblance already," she said.

Rick picked up the blanketed baby and carried him back to Amy, handing the baby to her and sitting down in the chair beside the bed. "You know, he's perfect, Amy," he said softly. "You're perfect. You did everything just perfectly tonight, you know."

Marsha nodded. "You really did, Amy. You couldn't have had this baby any better."

"Well, you both made it possible," Amy replied. "Thank you, Marsha. I wouldn't have wanted anyone else to deliver him."

Marsha blinked back stinging tears. "You know I wouldn't have let anyone else deliver him! Now, listen. I want you to put the baby in the bassinet over there after he nurses, then all three of you get some sleep. I'm sure you could all use it! I'll be by to check on you in the morning and if all goes well, you can go on home tomorrow. If either of you wants to make up for that supper you lost, the night nurse can make you some sandwiches. Rick, be sure to call Mama and Daddy before you go to bed and tell them they're grandparents."

Rick and Amy nodded. They both thanked Marsha

again and Rick continued to lavish praise on Amy as Marsha left the room. I swear, Amy has never messed up in her life, Marsha thought as she wandered slowly to the car. She can lie down and have a baby perfectly, and I can't even cook a simple dinner! How can one sister have so much talent and the other have so little?

Sliding behind the wheel of her car, Marsha slapped the steering wheel with the palm of her hand. What was wrong with her? Why couldn't she get her act together? Why couldn't she accomplish the simple task of cooking supper for Ward? She drove home in the dark night, stopping at a McDonald's that mercifully was still open at midnight and eating a Big Mac. She pulled into the parking lot of her complex and got out of the car, too wound up and frustrated to possibly sleep. Leaving on her uniform shirt but changing into a pair of shorts, Marsha dragged her shoe skates out of the closet and carried them down the stairs, sitting down on the bottom step and lacing them on. Maybe if she skated for an hour or two she could work off some of the frustration.

Marsha skated out of the parking lot and onto a sidewalk that skirted the apartment complex. Moving her feet rhythmically, she glided down the block and turned the corner, an unconsciously graceful figure dappled by moonlight as she skated the length of another block. Marsha could feel the tension easing as the soft night air blew into her face and lifted her heavy bangs off her forehead. Deliberately driving the disastrous dinner from her mind, she thought about the baby she had just delivered and how delighted Amy and Rick obviously were with their new son. He had weighed in at just over seven pounds, and already he looked just like Rick. Danny, you're a lucky boy to be born to those two, if you get your mama's brains along with your daddy's looks.

Smiling to herself as she thought about Danny, Marsha

skated down another block and around a corner, zipping by a small shopping center where she often shopped in one of the boutiques. Her mind on her small nephew, she barely glanced to her side as she skated into an intersection. Suddenly the glare of lights was upon her, a car coming from out of nowhere. Moving instinctively, Marsha dove for the other side of the street, managing to stay upright until she was out of the path of the oncoming car. But as she cleared the car, her skate caught on a small rock and Marsha went flying into the pavement, her palms outstretched.

Quivering with shock and fear, Marsha lifted her head and observed to her horror that she was still out in the middle of the intersection. Scrambling to her feet, she tried to skate to the curb but discovered to her astonishment that her knees were trembling too badly to carry her. She crouched and skated slowly to the curb, where she sat down and buried her face in her hands. Damn it, she could have been killed! Drawing her knees up, she laid her cheek on her knees and willed the rising nausea to go away.

Marsha sat for long minutes, her hands and her legs stinging. Finally, realizing that she still had to get back to her apartment, she stood up, noticing a dark stain in the street where she had been sitting. Looking down, she could see blood gushing from an open wound in her leg. Uttering a very rude word, she realized that not only would she be unable to get to her apartment under her own steam, but that the cut would require stitches.

Marsha sat down and unlaced the skates, then limped back to the shopping center, praying that she would find a pay telephone on the wall. Finding a single telephone, she dropped in her only quarter and dialed Amy's number, so numb that it took her four rings to realize that there would be no one there. Cursing softly, she retrieved her quarter and wracked her brain for someone to call for help, realizing that her only alternatives were to either call Rick at the birthing center or to call Ward. She started to dial the birthing center, but she hated to take Rick away from Amy tonight, so she sighed and dialed Ward's number.

Katy answered the telephone. "Hello," she said softly.

"Katy, this is Marsha Walsh. May I speak to Ward, please?"

"Oh, Marsha, he went to bed over two hours ago," Katy replied graciously. "May I take a message?"

"Katy, I hate to ask you but this is sort of an emergency. Would you wake him up, please?"

"Sure, are you all right?" Katy asked.

"Not exactly," Marsha said.

She could hear the sound of the receiver being put down, and in just a moment a sleepy-sounding Ward answered the telephone. "Katy said you were in trouble," he demanded.

"I am," Marsha admitted, close to tears. "I fell down and split my leg open, and Rick's with Amy, and I need to get to an emergency room. Can you take me?"

"I'll be right there," Ward replied.

"Wait!" Marsha cried. "I'm at the corner of Green Haven and College."

"You're *where?*" Ward asked.

"The shopping center on the corner of Green Haven and College," she replied patiently.

"That's what I thought you said," Ward muttered. "Let me get some pants on and I'll be there."

Relieved, Marsha sat down on the curb and buried her head in her hands, her hair spreading out like a curtain to cover her white face. Trembling, she tried to ignore the sting in her palms and the throbbing of her leg. Oh, God, I've pulled some stunts in my day, but this one takes the

105

cake, she thought. Nearly getting myself run over at one in the morning! I bet my guardian angel is one mass of bruises.

Ward sped through the streets of Austin, cursing under his breath every time he had to wait for a light. What had Marsha done to herself? Was she badly hurt? And what was she doing on the corner of Green Haven and College? He spotted the intersection ahead but searched in vain for the Monte Carlo. Where was she parked? He pulled into the parking lot and froze as he saw the small, huddled figure sitting next to a pair of shoe skates. "Good God, I don't believe it!" Ward said out loud. "She was *skating!*" He looked at his watch and whistled in disbelief. I could ring her crazy neck. At that moment Marsha raised her dazed, pain-filled face and all thought of punishment flew out of Ward's mind as he slammed on the brakes and got out of the car. Running to where Marsha sat, he pulled her up as gently as he could and held her close to him, rubbing his arms up and down her trembling body. "You're going to be all right," he crooned over and over. "I'll get your leg taken care of."

"Thanks for coming," Marsha said weakly. "Oh, I'm so dizzy!"

Instantly, Ward scooped her up in his arms and carried her to the Toyota, carefully placing her in the front seat. He picked up her skates, threw them in the backseat, and got in, pushing Marsha's head down between her legs when she started to pale even more. "Where's the nearest hospital?" he asked.

"Oh, a doc-in-a-box will do," Marsha said, her voice muffled against her knees.

"A what?" Ward asked.

"An emergency clinic," Marsha replied. "There's one just a few blocks west." She stuck her head up long enough to point out the general direction, then put it back down on her lap.

Ward drove to the emergency clinic without speaking, his free arm caressing Marsha's bent head. She protested, but he insisted on carrying her inside and sat her down in the waiting room. Fortunately the young doctor manning the clinic was free, and in just a moment Marsha was seated on an examining table, a vial of smelling salts reviving her.

The young doctor looked at her leg and whistled. "You put in a deep one there," he said admiringly. "That's going to take some stitches. How'd you do it?"

"A car nearly hit me," Marsha admitted as Ward's breath caught in his throat. "I was skating across an intersection and didn't see it coming. I had to dodge it and fell in the street."

"Oh, good night!" Ward muttered.

The young doctor looked at her as if he couldn't quite believe it. "You were skating?" he asked. "Isn't it a little dark out there for that?"

Marsha shook her head. "Not really. The moon was out."

Ward and the doctor exchanged glances, and the doctor washed out the wound. "Looks like a piece of wire was in the street," he said as he injected a needle of Novocain into the skin flaps. "Nice scar there," he commented idly as he waited for the Novocain to take effect. "Football knee?"

Marsha nodded. "Two months on crutches in the ninth grade and no tennis or racquetball ever again," she said regretfully.

"Oh, I don't think you're missing out on too many outdoor sports," Ward said dryly as he draped his arm around Marsha's shoulders. The doctor made quick work of the stitching and washed and wiped his hands with an antiseptic.

"Now, try to stay off that leg until morning, longer if that's possible. The stitches should dissolve in about a week."

"Thanks," Marsha said as Ward swept her into his arms and carried her to the waiting room. He pulled out his wallet and paid the clinic, then carried Marsha to the car and placed her inside.

Ward got in and started the engine. "I love that outfit," he said as he pulled out of the parking lot. "Are all the midwives wearing shorts to deliver?"

Marsha shook her head, too tired and achy to appreciate the joke. "I changed out of the pants when I got home," she said. "Amy had a little boy."

Ward's face softened in the moonlight. "Good for her," he said. He pulled up in front of Marsha's apartment and got out, carrying her up the stairs and waiting patiently while she inserted the key into the lock. He carried her straight to the bedroom and sat her on the edge of the bed. "Now I'm going to turn back the cover and put you under, and I'll sleep on the couch," he said.

"I need a shower," Marsha said as she looked down at her dusty, sweaty body. "I'm a mess."

Ward looked at her doubtfully. "You can't manage that," he admonished her.

"Please," she begged. "I can't sleep if I'm dirty."

"All right, I'll help you shower," Ward said. "Lift your arms."

Obediently Marsha lifted her arms. It occurred to her that Ward was going to see her with very few clothes on, but for some reason she didn't particularly care. He stripped off the dirty blouse and sweaty bra, then Marsha pulled down the running shorts, leaving herself clad only in a brief pair of panties that hid nothing. Ward scooped

108

her up and carried her to the bathroom, sitting her on the closed toilet while he adjusted the shower. "Can you manage in here?" he asked.

"I'll be fine," Marsha assured him.

"Well, call me if you need me," Ward instructed her as he left the bathroom. Marsha slid her panties down her legs and stared down at her battered legs and arms in dismay. She was going to be one mass of bruises in the morning! Standing, she swung herself into the shower and stood under the warm spray gratefully, letting the water wash away all the street grime. She soaped her body, gently cleaning the bruised places, and even washed her hair. When she stepped out of the shower she noticed that Ward had put a pair of her baby-doll pajamas on the counter. She stepped into the panties and pulled the top over her head, then she stuck her head out the door.

"I'm finished," she said.

Ward got up out of the chair and lifted her onto the bed, tucking the sheet in around her. "I brought you something to help you sleep," he said, handing her a snifter of brandy.

"Umm, this is delicious," Marsha said as she sipped the liquor. "Where did you get this?"

"I had it in my trunk," he said. "Here, want some more?" he asked as Marsha drained her snifter.

"Whasamatta, trying to get the lady drunk?" Marsha teased as she extended the snifter.

"Sure, that way I can rob you of your virtue!" Ward teased as he poured her another couple of fingers. "No, you're bound to be tense and hurting, and this will calm you down and ease the pain as well as anything I know of. Unless you have something in your medicine chest that you would prefer."

Marsha shook her head. "This is more fun than a pill,"

she said as she sipped the brandy. They finished their drinks in silence, their eyes meeting occasionally over the rims of the glasses.

Ward took the empty snifter from Marsha and set it on the nightstand. "Now, you slide under the covers and go to sleep," he instructed her. "You have a long day tomorrow, I'm sure."

Marsha nodded and slid under the covers. Ward reached out and touched her lips with his, meaning to kiss her for only a moment, but as her mouth opened beneath his, he gathered her close to him and drank freely of her sweetness. The tension of fear for her left him, to be replaced with the tension of desire. Yet he felt much more than just desire for this woman, he realized dimly as his lips moved against hers.

Marsha groaned and pulled him closer, her fingers knotting in the knit shirt that covered his body but did nothing to conceal the lean, wiry muscles beneath. Falling back into her pillow, Marsha took Ward with her, holding him on top of her as she welcomed his tender, passionate embrace. Tonight there was more than passion when Ward kissed her and caressed her. In spite of the pressure of his mouth on hers, there was the tenderness and caring in his touch that Marsha needed tonight. It had been so long since a man really cared.

Breaking his hold on her lips, Ward kissed each cheek gently. "I need this, Marsha," he whispered as he brushed the damp hair from her temple and kissed her there. "I need to hold you so badly tonight!"

"I need you too," Marsha confessed as she made lazy patterns with her fingers in the back of his shirt. "I need you to hold me, to touch me. I need you to care about me." Ward caressed her face and neck with tender, comforting kisses, and she made no protest when he untied the bows that held her pajamas top in place and lowered

110

it to her waist. The soft lamplight shone on her breasts, white against the dark tan of her bikini lines. For a long moment Ward looked at her body with reverent awe on his face as he observed her dazzling, petite perfection.

"Beautiful, so beautiful," Ward said as he bent his head and captured one small breast in his mouth, sucking it as Marsha moaned in pleasure beneath him. This was heavenly.

Desiring to touch him, too, Marsha raised her head. "Take your shirt off," she whispered. "I want to feel your chest against my breasts."

Raising himself slightly, Ward pulled his knit shirt over his head and threw it across the room, baring his chest to Marsha's eager gaze. A light sprinkling of hair touched his chest and arrowed down into his jeans. Marsha reached out and touched the hair, finding it surprisingly soft to the touch. Then Ward lowered himself almost to her, teasing her breasts with his chest until she was moaning.

"You're beautiful too," she said softly as Ward captured one breast in his mouth. He caressed it with his tongue until Marsha moaned in pleasure, her control on her emotions completely gone. "Make love to me, Ward," she whispered. "Now. Tonight."

"I don't think we better," he said as Marsha shifted her bad leg under him. The immediate shooting pain made her flinch. "See what I mean?" he asked softly. "I could hurt you, remember?"

"I guess you're right," Marsha agreed, the pain dimming but not totally dispelling the passion she felt. "And you need to get home to Katy."

Ward shook his head as he reached down and unzipped his pants. "I told her she could reach me here if she needed me. I figure that you need me more tonight than she does." He casually took off his pants and sat down on

111

the edge of the bed. "Do you mind if I sleep here, or should I make me a bed on the couch?"

"Here," Marsha whispered, staring at Ward's strong body clad only in briefs. "I need you beside me."

Ward climbed into the bed, then took Marsha in his arms, kissing her gently and holding her to his heart. They kissed long and lingeringly, Marsha feeling warmth and comfort rather than desire in Ward's strong embrace. In a few minutes, exhaustion and brandy did their work and Marsha was sound asleep, cuddling against Ward like a small kitten. He held her to him, desire for this woman licking him like fire. She was so infinitely desirable. It was all he could do to keep from waking her up and making love to her. Only the knowledge that he could hurt her leg stopped him.

Marsha cried out in her sleep and Ward held her close to him, patting her hair and whispering in her ear. It's been a long time since anybody took care of you, hasn't it, little one, he thought. And what on earth were you doing out on your skates at one in the morning? Ward shook his head in the dark. Tonight had not been the time to get after her about it, but he meant to give her a piece of his mind in the morning. She could have been killed.

Marsha swore as the alarm went off, then she reached out and slapped it off, suddenly conscious of a lovely warmth bathing her back. Blinking, she lay very still as the events of the evening before filtered slowly into her mind. She had tried to cook dinner for Ward and it was a failure. Then she had delivered Amy's baby, and she had gone skating by herself and fallen, and Ward had taken her in for stitches. He had brought her here and had held her as she slept, but he had not made love to her. And I

112

asked him to sleep here, Marsha thought as she turned a bright shade of red. I actually asked him to sleep here!

Easing out from under Ward's arm, Marsha crawled out of bed, wincing as a thousand sore places in her body protested. She tried her leg and found it stiff but not painful, which was a relief, since she had an office full of patients to look forward to all day. She pulled a pair of panties out of the drawer and fumbled around until she found her last two clean bras, both of which were bright purple. Grimacing, she found a dark enough blouse to disguise the purple bra, and as quietly as she could she crept into the bathroom and showered quickly, pulling on the panties and the bright bra and the dark blouse, then put on a little makeup, covering the dark circles under her eyes with a concealer. Promising herself that she would tackle the laundry this afternoon when she got home, she pulled on a pair of uniform pants and tiptoed into the kitchen. She started a percolator of coffee and made a stack of toast. Ward stumbled into the kitchen as she smeared jelly on a piece of toast. "Is that breakfast?" he grimaced. Marsha looked up to find him dressed, but his face unshaven and his eyes bloodshot.

"I'm out of almost everything else," she admitted. "Sit down and I'll pour you a cup of coffee." She took a second mug from the pantry and poured Ward a generous cup. "How do you take it?" she asked.

"Black," Ward muttered as she handed him the mug. He sipped it cautiously, letting the warmth and the reviving caffeine work their magic.

"Would you like a piece of toast?" Marsha asked as she poured her own cup of coffee and piled a plate high with the toast. She set a plate in front of Ward and sat down across from him, sipping her coffee and nibbling on her toast.

"I guess you know that was a damn-fool stunt you

pulled last night," Ward said heavily as he set his coffee cup down with a thump.

Marsha's toast froze halfway to her mouth. "I don't care to be lectured this morning, if you don't mind," she said, raising her toast to her mouth and biting off a piece with a definite snap. "I know it was stupid and I'm sorry." She knew that Ward was right, but she was tired and in no mood to be dressed down.

"Well, I don't give a damn whether you care to be lectured or not!" Ward replied with genuine anger in his voice. "What do you use for common sense, Marsha? You could have gotten killed out there last night! That car could have splattered you all over the damned pavement! How do you think that would make your parents and Amy feel?" And how do you think I would feel? he added to himself.

"I just couldn't stay cooped up in here," Marsha snapped, stung by Ward's honest words. "I'm more aware than you are that I could have been hurt badly or killed last night, so you can cut the heavy act right now. I don't need it."

"Well, you're going to get it. Of all the stupid stunts I've heard of in my years, skating around in the middle of the night does take the cake. Haven't you ever heard of rapists and murderers, Marsha? Doesn't that scare you?"

"No," she replied simply. "That fear has never crossed my mind."

"Well, I wish it would," he stormed. "Honest to Pete, woman, are you totally incapable of taking care of yourself? Do you need a keeper?"

"Damn you, Ward Sentell, why don't you just go on back to that paragon of perfection that you used to be married to and leave me alone if I'm so damned inadequate?!" Marsha cried, her eyes filling with tears. Damn him! If he thought she was such a failure, he could take

114

himself elsewhere. She picked up her coffee cup and plate and dumped them in the sink, then grabbed up her bag and limped out the door, tears streaming down her face. She shut the door with a resounding slam and made her way down the stairs the best way she knew how, smiling through her tears as a thought crossed her mind. Mrs. Gilbert would have a field day mothering her today.

Sentell, will you ever learn to keep your mouth shut? Ward asked himself angrily as he very carefully washed Marsha's cups and plates. He had thought that a lecture might do her some good, that maybe she would think twice before she went out alone in the middle of the night. Instead, he had obviously said something that had hurt Marsha deeply. She was not a crier, that much he knew, yet she was crying when she walked out of here.

It had to be more than the lecture about skating, Ward thought as he locked her door and started down the steps. She knew she deserved fussing at, and she would have never retaliated with that nasty crack about going back to Allison unless something had hurt her deeply. But what? What had he said or done to hurt her that way? All the way home, he went over the evening before and this morning's conversation, straining to remember everything that he had said or done, but for the life of him he couldn't figure out how he had hurt Marsha.

CHAPTER SIX

Marsha sat down in her desk chair and silently munched on her hamburger. Hal and Mrs. Gilbert had pressed her to join them over at the Seafood Palace, but Marsha's body ached all over and she knew she was feeling too morose to be good company today. Ward was right. She was incompetent; she did need a keeper. She finished off the hamburger and wadded up the foil and threw it across the room, missing the wastepaper basket by a good foot. See there, you can't even make a basket, she derided herself.

Marsha had gone by the birthing center and had released a very happy Amy and Rick. Amy carried her baby to the car with a smiling pride that was beautiful to see. And she'll make a wonderful mother, Marsha thought as she sipped the giant Coke that had come with the hamburger. If he were my baby, I'd probably stick him with a pin or lose him in the supermarket or something. But Amy will be great.

Marsha swallowed the last of her Coke as the telephone rang. The call could have been for anybody, but since Mrs. Gilbert was still out, she picked up the receiver. "Doctor's office," she answered.

"May I speak to Marsha Walsh, please?" Ward's deep voice asked.

"This—this is she," Marsha stammered, surprised to

hear from Ward. Why was he calling her after the nasty crack she had made to him this morning?

"Marsha, Katy just called me. She's having a few pains but nothing regular, although she says that they hurt and she sounded frightened over the telephone."

"Bring her in," Marsha replied at once. "They're probably false pains, but she's so close I don't want to take any chances with her. And, too, if I can get rid of that fear it will be worth a wasted trip for you."

"We'll be there in a few minutes," Ward said. He hesitated. "Marsha, are you all right?"

"I'm fine," she replied warily as she hung up the telephone. No, she was not all right, she hurt in a thousand places and she was an incompetent fool who couldn't even stay out of trouble, but other than that she was just fine! She brushed her teeth in the rest room and left a note for Mrs. Gilbert to send Katy in the minute she arrived.

Thirty minutes later she was facing a grim-faced Ward and a frightened Katy on the examining table. "It hurts, Marsha, it really does," she said. "They aren't all that regular, but when they do come they hurt."

"Have you been breathing with them?" Marsha asked as she donned a glove.

"I've tried, but it wasn't easy," the woman replied.

"Well, if this proves to be the real thing, we'll get you over to the birthing center and let you concentrate on your breathing." Marsha performed a quick examination. "Yes, this is the real thing all right, but you really aren't all that far along yet." Marsha turned grinning eyes on Ward. "Better call the university and tell them you won't be there this afternoon. You and Katy get down to the birthing center and I'll be along in a few minutes."

"With Amy gone there wasn't much I could do this

117

afternoon anyway," Ward replied, his tired face smiling a little. "Come on, sis. You're gonna make me an uncle!"

Marsha and Ward helped Katy down from the table and Ward left with Katy. Marsha saw two early afternoon appointments, then left, Mrs. Gilbert promising to reschedule the rest. Marsha got into her car and drove the short distance to the birthing center, thinking that if all went well they would be out in time for supper. Only she wasn't going to cook it for Ward tonight. If he wanted a fabulous cook, he would have to look elsewhere.

Katy was using the same birthing room that Amy had used the night before, the smell of fresh sheets and disinfectant in the air. She was dutifully breathing as Ward counted for her, a sheen of perspiration on her face. As Marsha looked at the girl, her professional instinct warned her that this was not going to be the same easy delivery that she had assisted last night. Hoping that her instinct was wrong, Marsha pulled on a glove and plastered on a smile. "OK, Katy, let's see how far you've come."

Marsha performed her examination, her optimistic smile fading inside even though her face did not change. "There's been no real change since you left the office," she told Katy, hating the way the woman's face fell. "But don't worry, sometimes we won't make much progress for a long time and then we'll make a lot of progress all of a sudden."

Katy nodded as another contraction came on her. "Now breathe with it, Katy," Marsha coached. *"In* two three four, *out* two three four. That's the way, Katy. You're doing fine." Ward turned worried eyes on Katy and Marsha reached out and patted his hand in a gesture of reassurance.

As the afternoon wore on, Marsha grew more and

more concerned. Katy simply was not making the smooth, steady progress that was needed to prepare her body for childbirth. Her contractions were sporadic, coming at irregular intervals, and Marsha suggested about four thirty that they should call Dr. Neimann in so that Marsha could administer a drug that would stimulate labor. Ward was agreeable but Katy objected violently, feeling that the drug would harm the baby. Marsha checked and found a strong, steady fetal heartbeat, so she agreed to wait for an hour or so before she called in the doctor. Ward objected but Marsha took him out in the hall and reminded him that going against the mother's wishes when it wasn't totally necessary could be very counterproductive in the long run.

As though Katy knew that she had to do something, her body soon went into regular hard contractions, the kind that usually sped progress along. Not so for poor Katy. Although the contractions were quite strong by now, her body was simply not making the progress needed to deliver a baby. Two hours went by, then another two, and Katy was not much closer to delivering than she had been when she came in. In spite of Katy's training, Marsha could tell that the pain was tearing the girl apart and wearing her out. So, ignoring her own personal preference not to use painkillers, she brought up the subject twice. The first time Katy refused outright.

At about nine Marsha brought up the subject again. "Katy, I know you wanted to go this delivery without medication, but you're worn out and you're about to lose control, and if you do that, we'll have to call in the doctor anyway. Now, I want to call Dr. Neimann and have him authorize a little Demerol."

"Do I have to?" Katy whispered, indecision flitting across her face. "What do you think, Ward?"

"I think you should have taken it the first time Marsha

suggested it to you," he replied as he held his sister's hand. "Please, Katy, you don't have to suffer like this."

Katy nodded as another pain gripped her. "I'll call Hal," Marsha said as she went to the telephone. Hal immediately authorized the medication and Marsha warned him that he might have to intervene in this one if Katy did not make any more progress in the next hour.

Somewhat relieved by the Demerol, Katy was able to stay in control and in the next hour she had advanced to the point where she could deliver the baby, but Marsha's examination revealed that Katy's baby was presented face first and that it was very large. She turned concerned eyes on Ward and Katy. "Katy, I don't think you're going to be able to deliver this one—it's turned wrong and it's simply too big. Will you—"

"No!" Katy snapped, exhaustion and pain taking away her control. "I want to have this baby!"

"But, Katy, Marsha knows what she's talking about!" Ward replied, pain for his sister showing on his face.

"Please, let me try," the tired girl begged. "I want to do this right."

Marsha checked for the fetal heartbeat, then laid a gentle hand on Katy's arm. "Katy, you know there's no right way or wrong way to have a baby. If it means that much to you, I'll let you try, but please don't be disappointed if you can't do this without help." Ward started to open his mouth but Marsha put her finger to her lips. "It won't hurt her to try."

Katy pushed for the better part of an hour, but the baby did not budge. Finally Marsha sat down in the chair beside the bed and took Katy's hand. "Katy, we're going to have to do something or you're going to run the risk of harming or losing your baby. You're just too little and that baby's just too big for you to have it normally. I'm sorry."

Katy looked at Marsha's face and started to cry. "But I want to have it naturally! I want to see it being born! I want to be a good mother!" She cried as another pain caught her in its grip.

"I know you do," Marsha said soothingly. "And being a good mother has nothing to do with whether you have the baby naturally or have it with help."

"Katy, Mom had all of us that way," Ward said. "She was too little to have us naturally."

"All right," Katy sobbed. "Oh, Ward, I wanted to do this so much!"

Ward took Katy into his arms as Marsha hurried to the telephone. She outlined the problem to Hal, who said he would meet them at the hospital in ten minutes. Ward wrapped Katy in a blanket and carried her to Marsha's car, since it was larger and the three of them would be more comfortable. Marsha rushed them over to the hospital and parked in the front driveway. She helped Katy out and gave her keys to the parking attendant. Hal had already called Admissions and Katy was instantly whisked to the labor suite, Marsha trailing behind her. Ward would follow as soon as he had tended to admitting Katy.

Hal was waiting for them in the examining room. A nurse helped Katy into a hospital gown and Hal checked her quickly. "Katy, there is no way that you can deliver this baby," he said with compassion, confirming Marsha's diagnosis. "I'm going to perform a Caesarian. Now, this will in no way affect your ability to nurse or to care for your baby in the next few days, but your recovery time may be a little longer. That's all."

Katy nodded, her eyes dry but filled with bitter disappointment. I've failed her, Marsha thought sadly as the nurses came to prepare Katy for surgery. She thought back over the last twelve hours. Was there anything she

121

could have done differently? Should she have tried to turn the baby? No, Hal would have recommended that if he had thought it would have worked. As surgically conservative as Hal was, if he thought Katy needed a Caesarian, then she did.

But I should have prepared her better for the possibility, Marsha derided herself as the orderly helped Katy onto the stretcher. We make such a big deal out of having a baby naturally that we put a guilt trip on those who aren't able to, Marsha thought as she followed the stretcher down the hall, holding Katy's hand and assuring her all the way to the delivery room that she was *not* a failure. Marsha scrubbed and gowned quickly, arriving back in the delivery room just as Hal made the first incision.

The birth was over quickly. A mere six minutes later Hal was holding up a huge, red-faced, squalling girl. "Thank goodness the baby's all right," Marsha breathed as she took the baby from Hal and wiped and examined her. She placed the baby in the incubator and wheeled her out to the corridor, where she would show her to Ward.

Ward sat up and stared at her in surprise. "That was certainly quick," he said. "What do we have here?"

"See for yourself," Marsha invited him. "I haven't put on a diaper yet."

"Well, how about that," Ward breathed as he looked down at the baby girl. "Kind of big, isn't she?"

Marsha nodded. "If the baby had been smaller, Katy wouldn't have had such a problem. It will be twenty minutes or so before Katy's out of surgery, then when the anesthesia wears off you can see her." She let Ward look at the baby for a moment longer, then she started to wheel the baby away.

Ward put out his hand and caught her arm. "Thanks, Marsha," he said softly.

Marsha's face twisted into a grim smile. "What for?" she asked. "I couldn't help her." She turned on her heel and wheeled the baby to the nursery.

She handed the baby over to the competent night nurses and shed her greens, turning her nose up at her rumpled uniform. Oh, well, she wasn't out on a date tonight! She joined Ward just as Hal stepped into the waiting room. "I assume you've seen the baby," he said to Ward. "Katy's worn out but otherwise fine."

"Can I see her?" Ward asked.

"Sure, she should be coming out of the anesthesia in just a few minutes," Hal assured Ward. "Marsha, it might be a good idea if you stayed and talked to her too."

"I had intended to, Hal," Marsha assured him.

They waited for just a few more minutes until a nurse motioned them into the recovery room. "She's awake. I thought you might like to be the ones to tell her what she had."

Ward and Marsha leaned over the bed, staring into Katy's exhausted face. "Katy, honey, you have a beautiful little girl," Ward said.

Katy nodded, her eyes filling with tears. "Is she all right?" she asked eagerly. "Did the medication hurt her?"

"Of course not," Marsha assured her. "She was out of there so fast that the stuff probably didn't even have time to get to her. She's perfect—I checked her myself. You did fine, Katy. She was just too big for you to have on your own."

"Did I really do all right?" Katy asked, tears trickling down her face.

"I haven't seen such a brave and gutsy mother in a long time," Marsha replied honestly. "Now, you better rest all you can tonight, because that baby's going to be hungry in the morning."

Katy nodded and shut her eyes. Ward bent down and kissed his sister's cheek, then he took Marsha's hand and they left Katy to rest.

"I had no idea childbirth could be that bad," Ward muttered as they walked out of the hospital. The parking attendant gave Marsha her keys and pointed out which row her car was in.

"It usually isn't," Marsha replied. "Katy had a real bad time of it tonight." She unlocked the car and Ward got in with her.

"If I could get my hands on the bastard that fathered that baby, I think I would kill him," Ward said as Marsha started the car. "She went through hell tonight."

"Well, you never know who's going to have that kind of time and who isn't," Marsha replied heavily. "If I had known the difficulty she was going to have, I never would have taken her on."

"Oh, Marsha, I wasn't blaming you!" Ward said quickly. "You did everything you were supposed to do tonight. It would have been the same if she had been laboring in the hospital, wouldn't it?"

Marsha nodded. "Look, why don't I go out and find us a couple of hamburgers?" Ward suggested as Marsha pulled up in front of the birthing center. "I'll be at your place in fifteen minutes."

Marsha nodded, too tired to argue. She drove home and stripped the clothes from her body, showering quickly and pulling on panties and jeans. Well, one more day without visiting the laundry, she thought as she pulled on the other purple bra and a white gauze shirt, too tired to care that the bra showed through.

Ward rang her doorbell five minutes later, carrying a feast with him. "Since the hamburger stands were all closed, I decided to do this right," he volunteered as he unloaded cartons of steaming Chinese food from a paper bag.

"That's super," Marsha replied as she opened the refrigerator and got out last night's wine. "Is this all right?" she asked. "I don't know about you, but I could sure use it."

Ward nodded, then looked at her bodice strangely. "They were all I had that's clean," Marsha shrugged as she got out knives and forks and a couple of plates. "Oh, that smells good! What did you get?"

"Moo goo gai pan and egg foo young," Ward said as Marsha got out the wineglasses.

Marsha picked up a carton and read the name of the restaurant. "Oh, this came from Amy's favorite place," she said as she opened the carton. "Hey, you got fried rice too!"

"I missed lunch and dinner both," Ward said as he sat down and started dipping moo goo gai pan out of the carton.

"I'll stay out of your way," Marsha teased as Ward piled his plate with the tasty vegetable dish. "Wouldn't want you to take a bite out of my arm."

Ward picked up the carton with the fried rice. "Get all you want?" he asked. When Marsha nodded he piled the rest on his plate. "So this came from Amy's favorite place," he mused as he carefully lifted out several egg foo young patties. "How did she do last night?"

"You would have thought she had had ten babies," Marsha admitted as she dug into her share of the egg foo young. "Short and easy labor and Danny looks just like Rick."

"Amy was lucky, then," Ward said. "I'm glad she had an easy time of it."

"Thank you," Marsha said quietly, nibbling on the moo goo gai pan. "That's very generous of you."

"She did that well, huh? Sometimes I think your sister can do just about anything she puts her mind to."

Marsha felt a momentary sadness. "As far as I know, she can," she said. "But remember, her baby weighed a good two pounds less than Katy's. If Katy's baby had been smaller, she would have been able to deliver normally. Was the father a big man?"

"College linebacker," Ward replied. "So how about Katy? Is she really going to be all right?" His hand clenched tightly around the wineglass.

Marsha reached out and patted his hand. "You can relax; she is going to be just fine. Almost one baby out of five is born Caesarian these days, and you don't see all those mothers lying around languishing for months! But she has had major surgery and she will have to take a little better care of herself for the first few weeks. For example, Amy can go back to work after three weeks or so if she wants to, but in Katy's case I'd recommend a good six weeks."

"Well, that's immaterial in her case," Ward said. "She's planning to stay with me until this year is up and then she'll probably go back and finish her master's. Mom and Dad can support her until she gets a job. Dad's a rancher and is, shall we say, very comfortable."

"Good, that's one worry that Katy won't have," Marsha said.

"Any other problems we can anticipate?" Ward asked as he polished off the last of the rice on his plate. He looked in all three cartons, but Marsha had left them empty. Without speaking she got up and handed Ward a loaf of bread and a jar of peanut butter. "Thanks," he said sheepishly as he grinned at her.

"Any other problems," Marsha mused. "Yes, but her

126

problems may be more mental and emotional than physical or financial."

"And what problems are those?" Ward asked as he smeared a piece of bread with peanut butter.

"For some reason Katy was absolutely determined to have a drug-free, completely natural delivery, and you saw how bitterly disappointed she was that she couldn't do that. Now, I'm not saying that it necessarily will follow, but she may be very touchy and defensive about the Caesarian and 'failing,' although I did my best tonight to assure her that she had not failed in any way."

"And how do you think she's going to act?" Ward asked, his eyes locked onto Marsha's.

Marsha was busy scooping up the last of her rice and missed Ward's intense look. "Oh, she will be very sensitive about the Caesarian, and, for heaven's sake, don't make a joke about it. She may not even want to talk about her delivery. You'll need to tread on eggshells."

"Like I didn't do last night and this morning?" Ward asked.

"Yeah," Marsha said without thinking, then her head shot up when she realized what he had asked and she had answered. Her face turned a fiery shade of red. "Yeah, I guess that's what I mean," she said as she picked up her plate and carried it to the sink.

Ward followed her with his plate and silverware. "I never meant to hurt you, Marsha," he said as she took his dishes and put them into the dishwasher. "And for the life of me, I can't figure out what I did say or do to hurt you that badly." He reached out and grasped Marsha by the shoulders, rubbing them gently with his palms. "Would you at least let me know what I said or did that was so hurtful?"

His eyes were beseeching, but Marsha turned away and started picking up the empty cartons. How could she ad-

127

mit that she was incompetent? It would sound so silly. "It's nothing, Ward," she mumbled as she stuffed the cartons into the trash.

"Bull—" Ward broke off the curse and took the damp sponge from Marsha and wiped the table. Then he took her arm and walked her into the living room, where he sat her down beside him on the couch. "It is something, Marsha," Ward objected. "Look, I like the way this relationship is growing between us. If something is bothering you, I want to know about it, because I don't want what we have to go out the window."

"You laughed at my soufflé," Marsha said.

Ward stared into her eyes, not a speck of humor on his face tonight. "I laughed at your soufflé. Yes, I did, because a two-inch-high soufflé is pretty funny. And if it had been anybody else's soufflé, you would have been laughing, too, and a lot harder than I was. So why couldn't you laugh at your own?"

"Because Jerry laughed at my cooking too. Every night for months, until I finally quit trying. He poked fun and he downright ridiculed it. I can't cook, Ward, but I was afraid to admit it to you, because all you ever do is brag about dear, darling Allison's great cooking and homemaking! She could cook like a chef and I bet she never wore a purple bra because all the others were dirty, did she?"

Ward stared at her, deadpan. "No, I can't say that she ever did," he admitted.

"See there?" Marsha demanded, tears welling in her eyes. "She was perfect—she could keep house and cook like a dream. Amy's perfect too—she has a brilliant career and she can lie down and have a baby like she's sneezing, and the kid's probably as brilliant as she is, to boot. I'm not perfect. I can't cook your stupid supper and I'm not brilliant and I can't even keep from falling down

128

in the street!" Marsha stood up and walked across the room, fishing a Kleenex out of the box on the television and blowing her nose loudly.

"Oh, no, is that what's bothering you?" Ward asked as he got up and put his hands on Marsha's shoulders, not letting her flinch away from him. "Look, I'm sorry I laughed at your cooking. If I'd known that it bothered you, I'd never have even asked you to cook, and if I'd known about Jerry, I sure wouldn't have teased you about the soufflé. Didn't you know that a soufflé is one of the hardest things to make? Allison was a senior in college before she got the hang of it."

"What does her being a senior in college have to do with it?" Marsha asked.

"She was a home economics major, for heaven's sake!" Ward replied. "Of *course* she could cook! She had a degree in it!"

"Oh," Marsha said.

Ward steered her to the couch and pushed her back down beside him. "Now, since you don't have a degree in cooking, I honestly don't expect you to be able to cook like she could. I was just wondering if you cared enough about me to have me over here. When you asked me I was delighted, because I figured you cared.

"Now, about all this other stuff you're worried about. First, I'm glad your sister is brilliant and I'm glad she can have a baby easily. But, Marsha, as much as I think of your sister, she doesn't have a smile that can light up the entire room when she walks into it. She can't with a few words allay the fears of a frightened laboring woman. You should have seen yourself today! You had Katy calm and me calm, and let me tell you, childbirth to me is not one bit calming! Sure, Amy is talented, but so are you. You are just as outstanding in your own profession as she is in hers."

129

Marsha shook her head. "Not really," she demurred.

"That's not what those two nurses I overheard at the birthing center were saying," Ward said smugly. "I heard one of them say you were tops and the other one agreed with her."

"Estelle and Maggie said that?" Marsha asked. "But you said I needed a keeper!"

Ward groaned. "Look, I was frightened and angry. Do you have any idea what finding you in that shape did to me? You could have been killed!"

"You were scared for me?" Marsha asked. "I thought you were just sore because I bothered you and cost you a night of sleep."

"God, no," Ward groaned as he caught her into his arms. "I was scared to death for you." He nuzzled his face into her hair.

Marsha snuggled close for a moment, the warmth of Ward's closeness penetrating her misery, but after a moment she pulled back. "But I still can't cook or clean or sew like Allison could," she explained. "You said you liked it when a woman displayed her domestic talents, and I don't have any."

Ward set her away from him and looked at her sternly. "Now, will you get it through your head that I do not, *do not* want Allison or her great and wonderful cooking and cleaning and sewing back! And I can assure you that you *do too* have domestic talents!"

"Domestic talents? What on earth do you mean?" Marsha asked as Ward's face took on a seductive leer. "Oh, you mean *those* domestic talents," she said, nodding her head.

"Uh-huh, those," Ward replied. "That's why I didn't want to go to my place, since Katy was there. I wanted a demonstration of those domestic talents."

Marsha wrinkled her face and scratched her head.

"Domestic talents. You'd like a demonstration, would you?"

"Absolutely," Ward replied. Marsha looked at Ward with sparkling eyes. With just a few reassuring words he had managed to rid her of the paralyzing sense of inadequacy that had plagued her for longer than she cared to admit. So if a demonstration was what he wanted, a demonstration he would get! Grinning wickedly, she got up off the couch and flipped through her record collection, finding an old LP that she had filched from Rick in a weak moment. Flipping on the stereo, she found the correct groove and in just a moment the blaring trumpets that hailed "The Stripper" came blasting out of the speakers. Marsha adjusted the volume and turned to Ward. "Your demonstration of the domestic talent of one Marsha Walsh," she said as she glided to a position just in front of him.

As the music went into the main theme, Marsha started to sway seductively with the rhythm, swinging her hips provocatively with the music as she stripped off imaginary gloves and threw them to the audience. Smiling sensuously, she turned her back and shimmied, then whirled around and sent one rubber sandal scooting across the floor. Ward's eyes grew wide as she swayed her body to and fro, her hair swinging provocatively around her face. Not missing a beat, she reached down and removed her other sandal, throwing it into Ward's lap.

I don't believe it! Ward thought a moment later as Marsha's blouse came sailing across the room and landed on top of her shoe in his lap. She honestly means to do a striptease for me! He watched with eager eyes as Marsha moved gracefully in front of him, rolling her hips to the beat of the music, pushing off first one bra strap and then the other. Her eyes smoldering, she let the bra slide down her breasts until it was barely covering her nipples, then

131

as the trumpets blared she snapped open the bra and flung it away from her, the garment of purple lace landing over a lampshade. The sight of her small, perfect breasts now unconfined made Ward's mouth go dry as he remembered the way they had felt and had tasted in his mouth last night.

I think he likes my talent, Marsha told herself as she watched Ward's expression go from amusement to amazement to desire. Her breasts bouncing free, Marsha bumped and bounced with the music, caught up in the erotic beat of the old show tune. As the driving beat continued, Marsha slowly and provocatively slid the zipper of her jeans down and, an inch at a time, lowered them over her hips and down her legs, letting the rhythm of her hips shake the soft denim downward. One leg at a time she stepped out of them, kicking them nonchalantly to one side as she swayed to and fro, clad only in a pair of lacy white panties. Drawing out the torture, she left them on for a moment while she let her shoulders and her hips gyrate with the syncopated, passionate beat of the music. Finally, as the bumptious tune began to build to a climax, Marsha inched her panties down just a little at a time until they were over her hips, then reached down and stripped them from her body, tossing them provocatively into Ward's lap along with the rest of her clothes. As the music came to an end she bowed, her hair swinging over her face, then she slowly danced toward the door of her bedroom, throwing kisses to an imaginary audience. On the last note of the song she disappeared into her bedroom, shutting the door behind her.

Marsha sat on the bed and laughed as she heard the sound of a single pair of hands clapping in the living room. The door of her bedroom flew open and Ward came inside, dangling her panties on one finger. "That

132

was a super entree you made there with your domestic talent," he breathed. "What's for dinner?"

"I am," Marsha replied boldly, stretching her naked body across the bed and arching her back with an unconsciously provocative thrust. "I'm dinner, drinks, and dessert."

"Sounds like nectar and ambrosia," Ward said as he fell onto the bed beside her, holding her naked body next to his and pressing her close to him. His jeans and workshirt were rough against Marsha's bare skin, but it was a pleasant roughness to her. "Open your mouth," he instructed her. "I want to taste the sweetness of you; I want the honey."

Marsha obeyed. Ward plundered her mouth, tasting the sweet tang within as Marsha gave of herself freely to this man. She clung to his shoulders, his muscles trembling slightly under her passionate grip. Their mouths clinging together, they lay for long moments, loath to break the link that their lips forged but knowing that they would share so much more in just a moment or two.

Ward pulled his lips away from hers but rained soft, warm kisses all over her face and neck. "Your skin is like velvet," he murmured as he feasted on the soft warmth of her throat. His lips, warm and moist, lit a fire everywhere he touched her. As his soft caresses drifted lower, Marsha arched her small body so that her breasts would be ready for him when his burning mouth found them.

Slowly his lips traveled toward their goal until they had found one tiny pink nipple. Ward's tongue snaked out and stroked the tip, caressing it into a small rosy button. "Oh, Ward, that's delicious!" she whimpered.

"No, you're delicious," he replied, his tongue tangling around the crest. Not satisfied with the conquest of just one breast, his lips traveled slowly to the other nipple and roused it to a similar state of desire.

133

Marsha's fingers reached out to caress Ward's hard chest but encountered instead the rough fabric of his workshirt. "Uh, Ward," she began.

"What is it?" he asked as he raised his head from her midriff, his eyes glazed with passion. "You're not having second thoughts, are you?"

Marsha laughed out loud. "Good grief, no," she said. "But in nursing school they told us, well, that you weren't supposed to wear clothes when you made love."

"Yes, I guess you're right," Ward said as he sat up and moved away from her body. Quickly he shucked his clothes and left them in a messy pile beside the bed. "Do I need to wear anything?"

Marsha shook her head and hopped off the bed. "The salesman left me some samples and told me to try them, but this is the first chance I've had," she said as she found the new contraceptive device she was looking for.

Ward took her hand and pulled her down on the bed. "There hasn't been anybody in a long time, has there?" he asked as he framed her face in his hands.

"No," she said. She swallowed and looked Ward in the eye. "How about you?"

"Not for a while," he admitted. "I don't take it lightly."

"I could tell," Marsha said as she reached out and kissed Ward full on the lips. Then she backed away for a moment and studied Ward's naked body. Long and lean, he did not have an extra ounce of fat anywhere on his frame; his muscles were hard and symmetrical. His tan disappeared just below his waist and did not reappear until halfway down his thigh, giving his nakedness a tender vulnerability. "You're spectacular," Marsha told him.

"Naw," he said, blushing a little.

"Yes, you are. As a former nurse I've seen my share, and I can assure you that you have one hell of a body!" She pushed Ward down on the bed and ran her hands down his body eagerly, greedily, wanting to touch the body that appealed to her so already. The soft hair that she had touched on his chest continued down to his stomach, and she let her fingers follow her gaze until she was probing the softness of his lower stomach.

"What are you doing?" Ward demanded. "I should be making love to you!"

"Oh, quit your griping and let me enjoy you for a minute," Marsha chided him, her hands caressing his stomach until it was quivering, then, drifting lower, finding his masculinity and touching it with bold, confident fingers. Ward moaned but made no more protest as Marsha caressed him tormentingly until he was almost at the brink.

"All right, my turn," she said suddenly, flipping over onto her back and looking up at Ward with teasing eyes.

"You're right, it is time that I returned this exquisite pleasure," Ward said as he bent his head to Marsha's body. He let his lips graze her breasts again, turning them into hard buttons of pleasure, then his touch drifted lower, caressing the soft flatness of her stomach. As his fingers found the warmth of her femininity Marsha gasped softly, his fingers painting an erotic picture on the canvas of her thighs. Don't stop! she thought as her limbs trembled with pleasure. This is beautiful!

As her lips parted with a sigh of pleasure Ward covered them with his own, his thigh gently nudging hers apart. When he was sure she was ready for him he entered her, probing gently lest he hurt her or startle her. Marsha welcomed him eagerly, the desire to be one with this man and to give him pleasure uppermost in her mind. As he started to move within her she matched his rhythm thrust for thrust as he slowly built a fire that would consume them both. Because of her training Marsha knew the mechanics of sex better than most people, but Ward was introducing her to a world of feelings and sensations that she had never even guessed at. As he moved slowly it was her pleasure he had concern for, not his own, and as he brought Marsha gradually to the peak of desire he murmured her name into the stillness of the room. As the stunning culmination came, Marsha arched her body and whimpered, Ward's name a whisper on her lips. Ward groaned and flinched, his hard body driving into hers as he, too, reached the zenith.

"Talented enough for you?" Marsha asked wickedly as Ward laid his head on her shoulder.

"Oh," Ward groaned as he held Marsha close. "I may not get out of this bed for a week! You're a hell of a woman, Marsha. I hope you know that."

"And you're a hell of a man," Marsha replied as she clung to Ward in the soft night.

Marsha came awake slowly, strong warmth against her back for the second morning in a row. Ward's still here, she thought as her lips curled into a smile. They had made love a second time last night, then had curled up together and fallen asleep in each other's arms, their bodies tightly entwined. Turning onto her back, Marsha found herself staring into Ward's smiling eyes. "Morning, sleepyhead," he whispered.

"How long have you been awake?" she asked.

Ward shrugged. "Long enough to find out that you sleep with your mouth shut and that you don't snore," he volunteered. "And to find out that I'd like to make love to you again."

"Sex fiend," Marsha teased even as Ward started to caress her under the thin sheet that covered them. "Oh,

136

that feels good!" she whimpered as Ward threw back the covers and found one breast with his tongue.

"Got to see if you're as talented in the morning as you are at night!" Ward said as his lips feasted on her naked breasts. The sunlight filtering in the blinds dappled their naked bodies as Ward tenderly caressed her stomach and her waist. "Oh, Marsha, stop that!" he groaned as her fingers found a ticklish spot on his anatomy and tormented it wickedly.

Marsha laughed. "No way, Ward. Oh, stop it! You're tickling me!" she squealed as Ward's fingers found the sensitive spots under her ribs. She reached under her head and pulled out the pillow, beating him with it until a couple of feathers escaped.

"That won't work, my lovely," Ward said as he tore the pillow from her hands and threw it on the floor. "I'm going to ravish you. Your virtue will be ruined. Hey, stop laughing! How can I ravish you if you're laughing?"

"Aw, shut up and ravish me," Marsha taunted.

If their lovemaking last night had been tender and moving, this morning it was rough and playful, yet no less satisfying than it had been before. Ward claimed Marsha with a strength that stunned her even as they came together. They laughed, they rolled together, they made erotic jokes as their passion swirled ever higher, taking them both on a whitewater rapids ride that knocked the breath out of them. As the trembling climax came they plunged together this time, spinning around on a free fall through space.

They lay together, spent. "It's Saturday," Marsha said tentatively. "Would you like to spend the day with me?"

Ward raised himself up on one elbow. "At least part of it," he said as he pushed the hair out of Marsha's eyes. "Boy, we wrecked your bed, didn't we?"

Marsha looked down at the crumpled sheets and

laughed. "I guess I better wash them too," she said. "Care to go to the laundry with me?"

"I tell you what," Ward suggested. "You do whatever chores you need to this morning and go see Amy and Danny if you want to, and I'll go see Katy and find out what my niece is named. Then we can go out to Barton Springs for a swim and picnic and back here for another domestic talent show tonight. How about it?"

"Sounds great," Marsha said as Ward gave her a quick kiss. He showered while Marsha cooked a quick breakfast and then ate a piece of toast and kissed her good-bye.

I love him, Marsha thought as she watched him bound down the stairs and climb into the Toyota. I've fallen in love with Ward Sentell. What on earth have I done?

Her eyes wide with shock, Marsha stepped back into her apartment and shut the door, flopping down on the sofa and staring into space. I have gone and done it. I love him. And I ought to be happy about it, but I'm not.

But as she stood up and began stripping the bed, she had to admit that a part of her was glad that she had fallen in love with Ward. She would have had to love him to respond to him the way she did last night, and she would not have wanted to miss that. And, then, Marsha had a loving nature.

But can I trust my judgment about him? she asked herself as she pulled the purple bra off the lampshade and put it into her basket of laundry. He seems to be wonderful. I can't see anything wrong with him. But, then, Jerry had me fooled, and Jack did, too, until I saw that picture. Is Ward any different, or is he waiting to spring a little surprise on me? And how will I even know until it is too late? Sighing, Marsha picked up her large basket of laundry and a box of detergent and staggered out the door, kicking it shut behind her.

138

CHAPTER SEVEN

Marsha peered over the rails of the crib and made a face. "Hi, Danny. Say hi to Aunt Marsha." She reached down and picked up her cooing nephew. "Ow, kid, that's my hair in your fist," she said as she reached down and disentangled a fistful of her hair from Danny's tenacious grip.

"Hey, that's quite a boy, Amy," Ward said as he reached out and took the baby from Marsha. "Good grief, he weighs a bunch! I do believe he's catching up with Bree."

Amy smiled proudly. "Well, at three weeks it's easy to tell how fast they're growing," she said. "He seems to get bigger every time I look at him. How's Katy doing anyway?"

Ward settled Danny on his shoulder and followed Amy and Marsha out to the living room. "Pretty well," he said as he sat down in the recliner. Danny stared around with alert little eyes as Amy and Marsha sat down on the couch. "Thanks to Marsha, she's pretty much gotten over feeling like a failure about the surgery and she's really doing well with Bree."

"Oh, I'm glad," Amy said. "Tell her hello for me. Now, about the collecting trip, do you think I should plan to go? I'd hate leaving Danny behind, but if you need me . . ."

"Don't be silly," Marsha replied. "You're still officially recovering from childbirth. Besides, you don't really want to go off and leave Danny, now, do you?"

Amy shook her head. "But, Ward, if you need help, I'll call Rick to come a day early and I'll plan to go."

Ward shook his head. "No, don't go off and leave a little baby like that. I can manage alone."

"But that's pretty hard to do, drive the boat and drag the crowfoot bar too. You need two pairs of hands," Amy exclaimed.

"How about if I took along some help?" Ward asked as he slipped his arm around Marsha's shoulders. "Marsha, are you free this weekend?"

Amy's eyes grew wide. "Well, Laurie has the beeper," Marsha said. "Sure, I can make it!"

At that moment Danny started to fuss. Ward stood up and handed the baby to Amy. "I think he's hungry," he said. Amy opened her blouse and Danny started to nuzzle for her breast. Latching on, he began to suck greedily.

"Ward, if you'll go into the dining room and get me those notes on the table, we can go over them now and save you another trip out here to the house," Amy said.

Obediently, Ward went to the dining room. "Are you and Ward lovers?" Amy whispered across the room, her eyes bright with excitement.

Marsha blushed to the roots of her hair. "Yes, well . . ."

"Good for you!" Amy crowed as Ward walked back into the room.

"I take it you approve," he said dryly as Amy blushed as red as Marsha had. She stuck out her tongue at her colleague and took her notes from him, holding Danny with one hand and the notebook with the other. As Amy and Ward went over their latest findings, Marsha sat quietly, thinking about the man who was seated beside her.

140

In the last three weeks she was sure that she had given away her feelings for him a dozen times—in her eager response when he would call her, in her delighted smile when he came bounding up the steps and knocked on her door, in the way she held him in the dark of the night. And he had given away his feelings too. There was love in his eyes every time he looked into her face. But neither of them had said anything about putting their relationship on any kind of permanent footing, and this suited Marsha just fine. She wanted to be sure, very sure, before she made any kind of commitment to Ward. Falling in love with him had been bad enough.

Amy and Ward finished their business in about twenty minutes, and she put a sleepy Danny down as Ward gathered up the material he would need to take with him on the trip. Amy came back into the living room and yawned. "I'll be glad when Rick gets back to town," she admitted. "I miss him."

"Oh, you won't be so lonely next week," Marsha said. "You're going back to work, aren't you?"

Amy nodded. "I'm ready too. I'm glad Rick understands. I couldn't love Danny any more than I do, but I'm ready to go back."

"I'll have the collections in your lab by the time you get there Monday morning," Ward teased. "Wouldn't want you to feel neglected."

Amy laughed as Ward and Marsha bade her good-bye. "So what am I going to do for you on this trip?" Marsha asked doubtfully as she and Ward climbed in the car.

"Warm my sleeping bag?" Ward offered.

"Besides that?" Marsha asked.

"Really, an extra pair of hands is always helpful on something like this," Ward said as he backed out of Amy's driveway. As he drove through the quiet streets he told Marsha a few of the things she could do to help him on this trip. Since they would be leaving the next afternoon, he offered to come up and help her pack for the weekend. A complete novice when it came to camping, Marsha welcomed his help, and in just a few minutes Ward had helped her select some things that would be good to wear on a trip such as this, mostly old shorts and sneakers and some long pants to protect her legs in case they had to wade through dense brush. He insisted that she pack a couple of see-through nighties, which he assured Marsha would be very practical at the campsite, a fact that Marsha seriously doubted. And he even asked her to model one for him, just to be sure, and the two of them were soon entwined on her bed making love, the packing forgotten.

Ward appeared the next afternoon in a borrowed pickup truck with a camper shell and a boat trailer behind. "Where on earth did you get the truck?" Marsha asked as she tossed her suitcase into the camper and hopped into the air-conditioned cab beside Ward.

"It belongs to the guy who made the grant for all this research," he said. "Boat too. This is the rig I used all winter."

"This is nice," Marsha said. They drove east through Austin and then away from town, through rolling farm country that was surprisingly green for the middle of July. "Is Katy going to be all right this weekend?" Marsha asked.

"Mom and Dad came in to see Bree and to stay with her," Ward said. "Thanks again for all the help you gave her about feeling like a failure."

"Thank you for all the help you gave me along the same lines," Marsha said as she scooted across the seat and gave Ward's arm a hug. Ever since the night she had talked to Ward, she had felt much better about her cooking and herself in general, but she still had grave doubts

142

concerning her judgment about men. She still was afraid to trust her own judgment. But I'm going to have to do something about it, she told herself as she and Ward drove through the countryside, farmed acreage alternating with grassy pastureland. If this relationship with Ward continued down the path it was taking, sooner or later she was going to be expected to make a commitment of some kind.

As Ward drove farther and farther into East Texas, the land became even greener, and the pines trees for which East Texas was justly famous began to appear. Marsha breathed in the tangy aroma blowing in through the air conditioner, the fragrance filling her lungs. "Nice, isn't it?" Ward asked.

Marsha nodded. "But, then, I like all kinds of terrain —mountains, desert, anything that's more than just flat old farmland," she said.

"Ocean?" Ward asked, cutting his eyes over at her.

"That's my favorite," Marsha admitted.

Ward nodded and smiled. "Mine too," he replied.

They stopped in College Station for supper. "Your last chance for a civilized meal," Ward teased as Marsha ordered a huge plate of fresh fried catfish. They drove on through the late evening sunlight, Marsha grateful for the daylight savings time, as it would be light until almost nine in the evening. They drove deeper and deeper into East Texas, the pines growing taller and thicker. Finally, as night was beginning to fall, they drove into the Sam Houston National Forest and paid the nominal camping fee, then Ward drove around until he found a campsite that was just a few yards from the shore of Lake Livingston, a dammed portion of the Trinity River. "We'll be in and out of here for the next two days, but at least we can enjoy the lake at night and in the morning," he said as he killed the engine on the truck.

"Kind of deserted, isn't it?" Marsha asked. They had driven past other campsites, but the last one had been about a mile back.

"Why do you think I drove this far?" Ward teased her as he got out of the truck. Shining his headlights on the campsite, he got a tent out of the back of the truck and with Marsha's help he quickly put it up, Marsha marveling at Ward's skill with the slippery nylon and the wobbling poles. As soon as the tent was up, Ward got a kerosene lantern out of the back of the truck and lit it so that he could turn off the headlights. "Don't bother with that," Ward said as Marsha started to unload a sleeping bag. "It's way too hot for that."

"Do you want the stove?" she asked as she crawled around inside the camper. "The suitcases? The stools?"

"All of that and the air mattresses," Ward instructed. "Leave the rest of that junk in there," he instructed as Marsha started to hand him a funny-looking bar with a bunch of short chains attached to it. "That's for tomorrow. But do hand me the ice chest."

Marsha handed him items one by one, then climbed out of the camper. "You know, I'm suddenly very hot and sticky. How about a swim?" she asked as she ran for the water.

"Marsha, wait, what are you doing?" Ward demanded, running after her.

"Going swimming," she explained as she looked back over her shoulder, catching her foot on an exposed root and crashing to the ground. Her face burning, she muttered a rude expletive as Ward picked her up and dusted her off.

"How about if I go get the lantern and we check out the old swimming hole before you go jumping in?" Ward asked. "This lake has been known to have water moccasins."

144

Sometimes it's nice to have a keeper, Marsha thought, shuddering.

Ward returned in just a moment, the Coleman lantern swinging from one hand. Marsha looked down and grimaced at the dirty, dusty mess she had made of herself. Ward took her hand and together they walked the rest of the way to the water, Ward holding the lantern aloft and walking a few feet in each direction, looking for snakes and other unwelcome creatures. "Looks clear," he said finally as he hung the lantern on the swinging branch of the tree. "Come on, let's go in!" he said as he started unbuckling the belt of his jeans.

"But—but the lantern's on!" Marsha objected. "You can see everything!"

"I've seen everything before," Ward teased as he unzipped and dropped his pants. "And so have you."

"Oh, not you," Marsha said. "But what if someone should drive by?"

"There're enough trees between us and the road to hide us," Ward pointed out. "And there's nobody on the lake." He shrugged out of his shirt and pulled off his briefs, exposing his naked body to Marsha's eager gaze. "Well? What are you waiting for?" he asked as he dove into the water.

"Absolutely nothing," Marsha said as she peeled off her clothes and laid them on the bank. "Although I still don't think we need the light." Naked, she whooped and jumped into the water, gasping as she submerged in the cool lake. She kicked to the surface, finding Ward right in front of her.

"This is why we need the light," he said as he bent to kiss her naked breasts. "I don't want to kiss a tree trunk or something." He angled her head back and covered her lips with his own, tasting the sweetness of her embrace. Opening herself to him, Marsha wound her arms around

145

his neck and pulled him closer to her, her wet breasts scraping his hard chest. The rocks were rough to Marsha's bare feet and the waves slapped her back, but she barely registered the sensations, caught up as she was in the delightful feelings Ward was bringing to her.

Ward released Marsha suddenly and stepped back, splashing her in the face. "You want to swim, so let's swim!" he said as Marsha retaliated with a splash that landed expertly in the middle of his face. They laughed and romped for the better part of an hour, the lamplight casting an eery illumination on their naked bodies and the small circle of water that they were playing in. Finally, totally exhausted, they swam to the edge of the lake and climbed out.

"So where're the towels?" Marsha asked as she looked around on the bank.

Ward shrugged. "I didn't think of that," he admitted.

"Some keeper," Marsha complained, sitting on a large flat rock and wringing out her hair.

Ward crawled up beside her. "We could walk back just as we are," he suggested.

"Just our luck we'd be met by a park ranger or a troop of boy scouts," Marsha said as she shook her head. They sat side by side on the flat rock, exchanging long, lingering kisses as the warm night air dried their bodies. Then they slipped back into their clothes and Ward took the lantern and they headed back to camp.

"Here, blow this up," Ward instructed Marsha as he handed her an air mattress. She blew it up while Ward blew up the other one, the effort leaving her slightly out of breath. "Where are you going with that?" he asked.

"Aren't we going to put these in the tent?" Marsha asked.

"No, too hot," Ward said as he spread a heavy canvas tarp across a smooth flat patch of grass. "The tent's just

146

in case of rain." He placed his mattress on the tarp and motioned for her to do the same. Then he covered both with a sheet, carefully tucking in the ends, and tossed two pillows on their makeshift bed. "Ta-da! The Hilton couldn't be any nicer," he teased.

Marsha smiled. "The bed may not be quite as grand here, but you don't get quite that skyful of stars over your head at the Hilton," she said as she started pulling off her clothes. She opened her suitcase and found one of the ridiculous nighties that Ward had requested and slipped it on.

Ward pulled her close and kissed her long and lingeringly. "Very nice," he said as he pulled Marsha down beside him on the mattresses. "And just the thing to entice the bears."

"Bears!" Marsha said, bolting upright. "Where?"

Ward laughed as he pulled her back down next to him. "You know, that's one of the things I love about you," he said as he kissed her lips. "You're so gullible. And so kissable," he groaned as he bent his head and kissed her, running his hands up and down the silky fabric of her satiny gown, her body lithe under the strength of his. "You're such a joy to kiss and hold."

Marsha's momentary annoyance at being teased melted under Ward's tender caresses. "Oh, I love kissing you, too, you idiot," she whispered as she caught him around the neck and pulled his lips down to hers. On fire, she rolled over on top of him, not breaking off their kiss until she was clearly in control. "And I love to touch you," she added. She unbuttoned his shirt and pushed it open, teasing the hard wall of his chest with her fingers, running them through the soft warm hair that had been her pillow for so many nights. Feeling him gasp lightly, she bent her head and nuzzled the warmth of his chest,

147

finding and touching one small, flat nipple with her tongue. "Do you like that?" she asked.

"I've liked everything you've ever done to me," Ward admitted as Marsha unzipped his jeans. "Here, let me get out of this stuff," he groaned as he sat up and quickly divested himself of his clothes. Pushing him back down, Marsha rained soft kisses down his chest and past his bony rib cage, rubbing her cheek against the soft firmness of his waist. Her lips continued their journey, finding his navel and circling it tenderly with her tongue. "Oh, Marsha, you don't know what you're doing to me," he groaned as her lips traveled even lower.

"So tell me, Ward. Tell me," she whispered as her lips found their erotic target and began to work their magic. Ward groaned and shifted, glorying in the touch and the tenderness of this woman. I love Marsha, he thought, not for the first time. She is so loving and generous with me. She does everything she can to bring me pleasure. She gives her all and holds nothing back. And her touch never fails to thrill me. Beyond rational speech, Ward let the excited moans from his throat give Marsha his message as she took him on a journey of delight, the erotic sensations filling Ward's being. Finally, as he was almost to the brink, Ward reached out and raised Marsha's head. "I can't stand any more," he whispered, pulling her slinky nightgown off her body.

She slid down beside Ward and opened her arms to him, letting him know by her actions that she was ready for his possession. But instead of taking her, Ward pulled back and looked into her face, his love revealed for her in his eyes. "I'm ready for you, Ward," she whispered.

"I know that," he said. "But let me make this special for you tonight." He lowered his head and touched her breast with the tip of his tongue, evoking an instant tightening of Marsha's nipple. He bathed that breast with his stimulating touch, then brought to her other breast the same delight. Not content with that, Ward let his mouth move lower, caressing her waist and her stomach with his lips and his tongue as she writhed beneath him. What a tender, loving man, what a wonderful lover, Marsha thought, to bring me delight like this. His mouth crept lower, loving her as she had him just a few minutes before, turning the core of Marsha's femininity into a quivering warmth of desire.

"Please, Ward," Marsha whimpered as his eager lips tormented her. "I don't know how much more of this I can stand!"

The stars in the sky twinkled their soft light into Marsha's eyes as she and Ward came together, joining their bodies and their hearts for a ritual that was as old as time but as fresh as the morning dew. An occasional cricket chirped, but other than that only the sounds of their loving broke the night's quiet. She whimpered a little as Ward set the pace, driving into her with gentle strength in a sensual rhythm that set Marsha on fire. Twisting and turning beneath him, she met his passion with passion of her own, her own excitement spiraling as Ward carried her on a whirlwind of pleasure to a place she had never been before, even with him. The stars in the sky were spinning when Marsha finally arched and called Ward's name, her body fragmenting into a thousand shards as pleasure ripped through her. Ward groaned and trembled, his own pleasure exploding in the dark night. Spent and satiated, they clung together as their whirlwind slowed to a breeze and finally to nothing, leaving them damp and drowsy in each other's arms. Ward pulled a sheet over their bodies and they slept, holding on to each other in the quiet East Texas night.

Marsha blinked as she felt a hand shake her shoulder. "Come on, Marsha, we have a lot of work to do today," Ward ordered her as she tried to pull her pillow over her head.

"Let me sleep," Marsha mumbled as she buried her face in the mattress.

Ward pulled the pillow out of her hands and rolled her over, the early morning sunlight dappling his freshly shaved face. "Come on, we have a lot we have to get done. A quick dip in the lake and you'll be ready to go."

"Kiss me," Marsha murmured, throwing her arms around Ward and pulling him closer to her, hoping that Ward would kiss her and forget about wanting her to get up.

Instead, Ward picked her up off the mattress and began to stride with her toward the water. "Ward, what are you doing?" she demanded as she came awake enough to have an idea what was on his mind. "No, you don't! Don't you *dare!*" she squealed as Ward tossed her naked body into the lake. Sputtering, she caught the bar of soap he threw in to her. "You fiend! I'll get you for this!" she threatened as Ward laid a clean towel on the flat rock and walked back toward camp.

Plotting all sorts of appropriate revenge for Ward, Marsha soaped her body and rinsed it quickly in the chilly water, wrapping the towel around her and rubbing herself dry. Thoughtfully, Ward had provided her with a pair of panties, cutoffs, and a sleeveless knit shirt that had seen better days. Her face curling into a grin, she pulled on her clothes and picked up her towel and the soap and wandered back to camp. "Are you sure I can be seen in the lobby in these?" she teased.

"Not in *my* hotel, madame," Ward laughed as he handed her a mug of coffee and a sweet roll. "Better eat a

150

couple of these," he suggested as Marsha made quick work of the roll. "It might be a while until lunch."

Before long Marsha and Ward were headed south, away from Lake Livingston and toward the undammed portion of the Trinity River. Marsha read the road map and determined where their best access points would be, and Ward turned off the main road onto a gravel county road that led past a number of fenced pastures. "I'll have to find someone who will give me permission to go on his land to access the river," Ward explained as he searched the area for a farmhouse. "Folks in Texas tend to be real touchy about trespassers on their land."

They found an old farmhouse at the end of the road and the grizzled old farmer was more than willing to let them access the river from his land, although his manner clearly showed that it was beyond him why a couple of city slickers would want to go mussel hunting in his river. Ward bumped across his pasture and parked, and together they pushed the small fishing boat into the water. Ward retrieved the funny-looking pole from the camper and got out a box of peculiar-looking hooks. "This is a crowfoot bar," he explained as he started hooking the small hooks onto the chains extending the length of the small pole.

Marsha watched him attach a couple of hooks, then she started hooking them on the other end. "What will this do?" she asked.

"As soon as we're done here, you're going to troll the boat very slowly, and I'm going to drag this pole across the bottom. The mussels will clamp shut on the prongs of the hooks and we'll pull them up. This is about the best way of getting them up, excluding diving." In just a moment the pole was ready and Ward threw it out the back, holding on to the rope. "Now, fire the engine and troll real slowly for about a hundred yards."

Marsha fired the engine and very cautiously pushed down the throttle. "Too fast," Ward said as the boat lurched. Marsha immediately pulled back on the throttle and Ward nodded. She trolled down the river until Ward told her to stop, then helped him pull up the bar and marveled to find several mussels of various sizes tightly clamped to the hooks. Ward started pulling them off and dropping them into bottles of preservative. He handed Marsha a grease pencil and told her to write Trinity River–July 1984. "Hey, what's this?" he crowed as he pulled off the last mussel. "This is a *Cyrtonaiasis tampicoensis.*"

"Is that like the ones that Amy gets all excited about sometimes?" Marsha asked, dropping the exciting mussel in the jar with all the rest.

"Sure is. This is about its upper geographical limit," Ward said. "Good haul—we have some *Quadrula,* a couple of *Anodontas, and a Lampsilis.*"

"Do I need to write all that down?" Marsha asked.

Ward shook his head. "Just help me get this bar back out in the water," he said as he hoisted the long bar.

He and Marsha trolled that small section of river for at least two hours, Ward delighted with the samples they were bringing back and Marsha delighted because Ward was delighted. They then got the boat out of the water, stored their samples in the camper of the truck, and thanked the cooperative farmer. About fifteen miles south they repeated the process, finding another farmer willing to let them have river access. Here they trolled for an hour or so and broke for lunch, feasting on thick ham sandwiches and Ward's mother's homemade pickles. They then trolled that section of river for another hour, finding fewer mussels than they had at the first site but certainly enough so that this stop was not wasted.

It was after three when they left the second site. They

again drove south, spotting a run-down farmhouse that was fairly close to the river. Ward pulled up in front of the house and knocked on the door.

After a few minutes the window shade fluttered, then a suspicious-looking old woman pulled up the shade. "What you folks want?" she asked.

"I'm from the University of Texas biology department. . . ." Ward began.

"Didn't ask for no cre-dentials, asked what you want," the woman broke in.

"Can I get my boat onto the river from your land?" Ward asked. "We're making some . . ."

"Suit yourself," the woman replied, dropping the shade and closing the window.

"Look at all the talking she saved you!" Marsha giggled as Ward got back in the truck. They drove to the edge of the river and parked the truck, but just as Ward started to push the boat into the murky water she reached out and pointed to an object close to his feet. "What's that?" she asked innocently.

"Oh, my God!" Ward said as he jumped about a foot off the ground. Taking Marsha's arm, he shoved her toward the cab of the truck and pushed her in, coming in right beside her. "That, my dear, is the *very recently* shed skin of a six-foot-long rattlesnake."

"Ugh," Marsha replied. She turned worried eyes on Ward. "But what are you going to do about collecting mussels along here?"

"Do you see any mussels?" Ward asked. Marsha shook her head. "I don't see any mussels either. So there must not be any mussels here, right?"

"Uh, right," Marsha laughed as Ward started the engine.

Since it was really too late to drive any farther south, she and Ward returned to camp, Marsha immediately heading for the cool lake to rinse the sweat from her body. Ward joined her there and they played and splashed for an hour or more in the late afternoon light. Marsha's face and arms were sunburned and Ward's nose was distinctly red, but neither of them really noticed or cared. Ward produced steaks from the ice chest, and charcoal and a portable grill from the camper, bringing down on his head a spate of teasing from Marsha about "roughing it" in the wilderness. He invited her to cut up a salad while he grilled the steaks, and they sat down together to a delicious dinner as the sun slowly lowered itself to the earth.

"Thanks for all the help today," Ward said as he polished off the last of the steak. "You really made the collecting much easier."

Marsha smiled into the darkness. "Sorry I can't be of more help in the thinking part of it," she teased. "In my line of work I'm called on only to identify boy and girl."

Ward laughed. "Do you always get it right?" he asked.

"Oh, absolutely," she said. "You see," she started to explain.

"Is *that* the way you do it?" Ward asked, pretending astonishment. "And here all this time I thought it was something mysterious!"

Marsha laughed. "You really like your work, don't you?" he asked.

"Yes, I love it," Marsha admitted. "But you knew that already, didn't you?"

"Yeah, I did," he said. "But for some silly reason I just like to hear you say it. But is it something you can do only in Austin?"

"Oh, goodness, no," Marsha said as she chewed the last bite of her steak. "The demand's springing up all over the country. I chose Austin deliberately."

154

"But are you committed to staying in Austin forever?" Ward asked.

Marsha shrugged. "Not necessarily. I could move occasionally, but I don't want to make a habit of it. It takes time to build a practice." She looked at him sharply but his head was bent into his plate. "Here, let me take that," she said as she picked up Ward's plate. She washed the dishes in a tub of soapy water and wiped them dry, then she and Ward wandered down to the lake, sitting on "their" rock and holding hands and staring up at the stars in the dark night sky, talking about everything yet nothing. Then Ward reached out and kissed her lightly on the lips, the brief spark kindling the flame of desire in Marsha that was never far from the surface when Ward was near. One light kiss became two, then four, and before long Ward was carrying her back to camp.

They spread their bed under the stars and came together again, their bodies seeking the pleasure that only the other one could give. With eager fingers they undressed each other, tossing their clothes in an untidy heap beside the Coleman lantern. Ward bent down and turned down the light until it was only a soft glow in the night. Then with a love and tenderness Marsha had only dreamed of finding in a lover Ward laid her down and proceeded to make her his. He covered her breasts and her stomach with warm kisses, finding and exploring all the intimate places until Marsha thought she would faint with pleasure. Knowing what gave Ward pleasure, her hands touched him and stroked him until he was groaning above her.

Hands and lips having done their work, Ward and Marsha became one yet again, touching and seeking and loving as their bodies united. How does he bring me this pleasure? Marsha asked herself as Ward reached down with his fingers and caressed her even as he possessed her

155

body with his own. Twisting in a frenzy of pleasure, the pressure between them built as Ward expertly brought them both to the peak of their desire. As they crashed together into the waves of oblivion, Marsha heard her name on Ward's lips even as she called out his name.

"You know I love you, don't you?" Ward asked as Marsha cradled her head on his shoulder.

"Yes, I've known for some time," Marsha admitted as she reached out and traced light patterns on his chest with her fingers. "And you of course know by now that I love you too."

"Yes, I do," Ward said as he sat up and pulled Marsha up with him. "You aren't very good at keeping a secret."

Marsha blushed, her face glowing in the dim light of the lantern. Ward reached over and turned up the lantern a little, its white glow brightening their naked bodies. He reached out and took her hand. "Marsha, I want you to be my wife."

I was afraid of this, Marsha thought as she stared into Ward's strained, earnest face. He's ready for a commitment, and if the truth be known, I am too. But can I trust my judgment about him?

She licked her lips and bit the end of her tongue. "Are —are you sure?" she stammered. "Marriage is such a big step. Wouldn't you rather live together first?"

Ward shook his head. "No, if I had wanted to live with you, I'd have asked you to move in and let it go at that. Marsha, you're not the live-with-a-person type, and neither am I. I want to marry you."

Oh, no, what could she say? Sorry, Ward, I'm afraid you'll turn out to be a dud? I can't trust my own judgment? I'm scared because I love you so much? She stared over at Ward's lean face, the lines in it softened with love for her. I do love him, she thought. I love him a lot. And

156

he honestly does seem different from all the rest. You have to take a chance on him, Marsha. You love him too much not to.

Marsha smiled and gave Ward's hand a squeeze. "If you honestly think that I'm what you want, then I'll be glad to be your wife," she said.

"Yes, you're what I want, purple bras and all," Ward assured her. He put his finger to Marsha's lips as she would have opened her mouth. "I love purple bras, especially when they end up across the lampshades." He leaned over and kissed Marsha tenderly, then got up and opened the ice chest, his nakedness so appealing. "I hoped you might say yes, so I brought along something with which to celebrate," he explained as he withdrew a bottle of champagne and two paper cups. He unscrewed the wire and the cork disappeared somewhere into the night.

"I guess we'll have to finish the bottle," Marsha laughed as Ward filled up a cup for her.

"I guess we will," he said as he sat facing her, cross-legged, sipping his champagne. "To us!" he said, holding his cup to hers.

"To us," she replied, touching his cup lightly and sipping her champagne. Oh, Ward, I hope I'm right this time, she thought as she savored the sweet, dry tingle of the bubbles that tickled her throat.

That was certainly a wonderful weekend, Ward thought as he reluctantly drove away from Marsha's apartment. Fifteen jars of specimens and a beautiful fiancée too! Ward smiled as he thought of what Marsha's reaction would be if he ever said that out loud. She would wring his neck! What a woman, he thought. And she loves me. She loves me a lot. Sentell, you are lucky.

He pulled onto the expressway, humming to himself as

he sped toward home. He had a telephone call to make, and he wanted to reach Wanda before she went out for the evening. She'll be glad to hear that everything's squared away, he thought. She's wanted me for a long time now, and she's about to get me.

158

CHAPTER EIGHT

"The ring's beautiful," Marsha said as she held out her left hand and admired the sparkling diamond in the simple solitaire. "Thank you, Ward."

"My pleasure," he said as he picked up her hand and kissed it, the touch of his lips on her fingers warm and reassuring. "I'm sorry I couldn't get it for you earlier this week, but I had to shift a little money around."

"You didn't have to spend so much," Marsha said as Ward started the car. "I could have worn a smaller one."

Ward shook his head emphatically. "No, you're going to be wearing it every day for the rest of your life. I want you to have something nice."

"I appreciate it," Marsha said as she reached over and kissed Ward on the cheek. I sure hope I'll wear it for the rest of my life, she thought as Ward drove toward her apartment, stopping by a drive-through Mexican food place and picking up a bag of tacos. I love him so much. But is there something about him I still don't know?

Marsha and Ward made quick work of the tacos and were soon sprawled across Marsha's bed, raising each other to the heights yet again. The rest of my life, Marsha thought as tremors of pleasure ripped through her when Ward brought her to the peak. Oh, Ward, I hope so, I really do.

Ward settled down next to her on the bed. "So when

159

would you like to get married?" he asked as Marsha snuggled closer to him.

"Just whenever," Marsha said.

"Around the fifteenth of August?" Ward asked.

"That's just a month away!" Marsha exclaimed, sitting up and looking down at Ward incredulously. "That—that's so soon!"

Ward's eyes narrowed. "Don't you want to marry soon?" he asked.

"Of—of course," Marsha stammered. "It's just that it takes time to get even a small wedding ready. We have to send out invitations, get a church, get dresses . . ."

"So get Amy to help you," Ward suggested. "And Rick can help you too. He once told me he's photographed over two thousand weddings, so he'll know what we need. And I'll do my share of it, of course."

"You know, Sentell, if I didn't know better, I'd think you really want to marry me," Marsha said as she folded her arms and looked at him.

"You know, Walsh, I really do," he said, pulling her back down into his arms and kissing her. He released her and climbed out of bed, pulling on his pants. "I'm tired of driving home alone at midnight."

"You just want to save gas," Marsha teased as she stuck out her tongue at him.

"That too," Ward said as she threw a pillow across the room.

Marsha pulled on a robe and walked Ward to the door, watching him as he bounded down the stairs and climbed into his Toyota. She held out her hand and stared into the sparkling diamond. He would have to love me to buy me something this elegant, Marsha thought as Ward's tail-lights disappeared into the night. Surely he's really all right. Surely I can trust my judgment this time. Shrugging her shoulders, Marsha shut the door and climbed

160

into bed, climbing out five minutes later to go to the birthing center and deliver a strapping set of twins.

Marsha parked in front of the biology building and hopped out of her car. She was hoping to catch Ward before he left and make sure the church she had reserved was large enough, and she also wanted to show Amy the ring. Striding into the building, she zipped down the stairs and into Amy's basement laboratory, spotting her sister bent over a sample bottle. "You never get through here, do you?" Marsha teased.

Amy looked up and blinked tiredly. "Uh, it doesn't look like it, does it?" she said shortly. "So what can I do for you?"

"Well, you can admire this," Marsha said, sticking her left hand up into Amy's face. "Ward gave it to me last night."

"Oh, Marsha, it's beautiful," Amy breathed. "It's official, then?"

Marsha nodded. "The fifteenth of next month," she said. "Ward said that maybe you and Rick could help us a little with the arrangements—not do the actual work, but Rick will know better than we do what needs to be done."

Amy smiled faintly. "If you're not careful, he'll take over the whole show." She sighed. "Sure, we'd be glad to help." She reached around and rubbed her stiff neck. "Did you want to see Ward too?" she asked.

Marsha nodded, then stared at what appeared to be tears in Amy's eyes. No, it's just my imagination, she told herself. Amy wouldn't cry for no reason. Amy's fine. "Has he gone home?" she asked.

"No, he went down to the faculty lounge for a few minutes, but he should be back soon. You can wait in his office."

"Thanks, Amy, I'll wait for him there," Marsha said as she rushed out of the lab, slowing herself a little at the door so she would not mow anyone else down in the hall. She found the door marked DR. SENTELL and pushed it open, wondering for the hundredth time how a scientist as methodical as Ward could be so messy at the same time. She plopped down in one of the lightly padded armchairs and stared around the office.

Ward is certainly taking his time, Marsha thought impatiently as she fidgeted around on the uncomfortable chair. She had been sitting there at least fifteen minutes and Ward still was not back. Oh, well, maybe he had gotten into one of his long-winded environmental debates with someone from the philosophy department. Since she was in no real hurry, Marsha decided to go ahead and wait for him, even if he took a while to get there. Maybe I can find a magazine to kill the time, she thought as she stood up and wandered over to the table that sat beside the desk. Flipping through the stacks of books, she could only find a lot of boring textbooks and a couple of issues of *Scientific American.* Maybe he has something in his desk, she thought as she crossed over to the large oak desk and started to open a drawer.

She spotted a letter that had UNIVERSITY OF NEW MEXICO as the return address. Hesitantly, she reached out and picked up the envelope, noting that it was dated just the day before yesterday. It's none of my business, Marsha thought as she went to lay the letter down again. But the file sat just a bit too close to the edge of the desk and her slightly clumsy fingers knocked the file and the letter to the floor, spilling the contents out all over the faded tile.

Klutz! Marsha chided herself as she picked up the letter nearest her feet, and she glanced down at it in curiosity. But her fingers froze halfway to the file as she glimpsed the phrase HAVE ENJOYED THE LAST SIX YEARS, BUT . . . But what? she asked herself as she started the letter from the top.

Marsha sat down in Ward's desk chair five minutes later in a state of shock. It was a carbon copy of Ward's letter of resignation from the University of New Mexico. She read the entire first page carefully, then read it again just to be sure she had read it right the first time. Yes, it was a carbon of a letter of resignation and it was on Ward's stationery. Her fingers trembling, she picked up the letter from New Mexico and read it also. It wished Ward well and hoped that he would continue to progress professionally. Not daring to read any of the other letters in the file, Marsha picked them up with unseeing eyes and put them back into the folder. She very carefully placed the file back on the desk and the letter from New Mexico on top of it, just as she had found it, then she squared her shoulders and dried her eyes and walked to the flight of stairs at the end of the hall and climbed them resolutely. Upon reaching her car, she turned the ignition and drove home, her movements automatic as the awful truth took its painful time sinking in.

Ward had quit his job. Plain as that. He had quit a perfectly good job, just like Jerry had done so many times in their brief marriage. Swallowing back tears, Marsha parked her car and climbed the stairs to her apartment, slamming the door shut behind her. I was right, she thought as she flopped down on the couch and buried her head in her hands. He does have a flaw. Same flaw your last husband had, in fact. You picked another loser, Marsha. You have landed yourself another dud.

How could he do this to her, when she loved him like she did? Letting the tears fall in the privacy of her living room, Marsha acknowledged to herself that breaking up with Ward was going to hurt her worse than breaking up

163

with Jerry or Jack. She was going to have to tear out her soul tonight when she gave back the ring and told Ward it was off. This time she had loved completely, fully, giving her heart and her soul to this man. And she had to break it off. There was no way Marsha could marry Ward knowing that she was about to go back on the merry-go-round that she had ridden with Jerry. Her spirit could not take that again.

Marsha's tears had dried and her face was calm when she let Ward in at eight, only a sadness around her eyes giving away her heartbreak. "Did you find a church yet?" Ward asked as he pulled Marsha to him and kissed her eagerly, Marsha's lips and heart responding to Ward's embrace even as her mind knew that their relationship was over.

Marsha pulled away from Ward and motioned him to the couch, but instead of sitting down beside him she stood nervously by the window, her hands folded across her chest. "I think we should call it off, Ward," she said softly.

"What did you say?" Ward asked.

"I said that we should call it off," Marsha repeated.

"Why? Couldn't you get the church?" Ward teased.

Marsha whirled around to face him. "I wasn't trying to be funny," she snapped as her eyes filled with tears. "I said that we should call if off."

Shock and anger warred on Ward's face as he registered the fact that she was not teasing. "You weren't kidding just now? You honestly want to call it off? You can't be serious!"

"I am, Ward," Marsha said.

"Give me one good reason," he demanded.

Marsha had her reason ready. "I've been thinking about another marriage, and I don't think I'm ready for that kind of commitment again," she said, hoping that

Ward would buy her excuse and not probe into the real reason why she didn't want to get married again. "I feel trapped."

"That's ridiculous!" Ward thundered. "You are not trapped. Getting married to me would not be a trap."

"Yes, it would," Marsha insisted. "Getting married to anyone would be a trap. I'm not ready for that."

"That's a bunch of sixties rhetoric that you've thought up to hide the real reason you suddenly don't think you want to marry me, and I won't buy that, Marsha," Ward ground out. "Look, you love me. I can see it in your eyes, feel it in your touch. And I love you. I want to marry you and be with you. And yesterday you wanted the same thing from me. So what happened to change your mind, Marsha?"

Oh, no, he had seen through her excuses. And I can't tell him the truth, Marsha thought. I simply can't bring myself to tell him that I know he quit his job. It would kill me to hear him lie about that to me. I'm sure his glib excuse is ready. Biting her lip, she shook her head sadly. "I really can't tell you, Ward, except to say that I think we both made a big mistake jumping into this engagement. We don't know each other well enough to contemplate marriage."

"You're going to have to do better than that, Marsha. Is it nerves? Are you afraid of getting married again?"

Marsha shook her head. "Oh, Ward, can't you accept this from me? Can't you let me end this gracefully?"

"No, I sure as hell can't!" Ward replied as he strode back and forth across the floor, hurt and defeat written all over his face. "We had something good, something precious. Think about last weekend, Marsha. That was wonderful. And not just the sex—we talked and we laughed and we loved each other. And now you want to break it off and you won't even tell me why, and you expect me to accept it gracefully! Marsha, how can I?"

Marsha sniffed as huge tears welled in her eyes and ran down her cheeks. "I just can't talk about it tonight," she whispered. She twisted off her ring and held it out to him.

"Put that back on," Ward commanded her harshly. "And don't take it off again until you can sit right there on the couch and give me a reason, a good reason, why we should break this off." He reached out and brushed a tear off her cheek. "Think about it some more, Marsha," he pleaded as he pushed the ring back on her finger. "Remember last weekend and think that our lives could be like that all the time. Please, don't do anything tonight." He reached out and kissed her cheek, then turned and walked toward the door. "We'll talk again in the morning. I hope you feel that you can be honest with me then." He pulled open the door and walked out of Marsha's apartment, leaving her standing in the middle of the room with tears streaming down her face.

Why has Marsha changed her mind? Ward asked himself over and over as he drove home. What reason could she possibly have for changing her mind? She was so happy when we picked out her ring yesterday! His thoughts returned to the weekend they had shared and his face clouded with confusion. She had been happy with him on the trip. In fact, she had seemed so happy with him ever since they had become lovers. Surely she wasn't still worried about Allison!

Ward pulled up into his driveway and stared out into the dark night, clouds obscuring the light of the moon and stars. Had he blown it again? He had chosen one woman who had turned around and left him. Had he chosen another who would do the same? Maybe it was nerves on her part, maybe—oh, what the hell, he would try to find out more in the morning.

Marsha flinched as the door shut behind Ward, then she collapsed onto the sofa, tears streaming down her face. I don't want to lose him, she thought as her fists curled around the throw pillow. Could I possibly marry him, knowing he's always going to be dependent on me? Oh, why can't I ever fall for a man who is all that he seems to be? Why do I always fall for the stinkers?

Marsha cried until she was spent, then in spite of the fresh scar on her calf she got her skates out of the closet and carried them down the stairs, strapping them on and skating through the warm summer night. What should she do? She could confront Ward with the truth and let him try to lie his way out of it if he cared enough to do so. Or she could keep coming up with excuses until he gave in and took back the expensive ring that he never should have bought in the first place if he was going to be out of a job. But he had looked so hurt tonight when she had tried to break it off. Was it possible that he wasn't another loser? But if he wasn't, why was he resigning from his job?

Marsha skated through the neighborhood for nearly an hour and a half, but she was as confused as ever when she finally sat down at the foot of the stairs and unstrapped her skates. Well, Marsha, let's see what you do with this one, she thought as she carried her skates up to her apartment and stowed them in the closet. She stripped off her sweaty clothes and stepped into the shower, standing under the warm spray for long minutes, waiting in vain for the pounding water to calm her trembling nerves. After a while she gave up and climbed out of the shower, catching a glimpse of her engagement ring in the mirror and wincing a little at the reflection.

hot sauce, *knowing* that she would get heartburn from it. She kept me up all night that night!"

Marsha laughed until tears ran down her face at this side of Amy. "I guess I've missed a lot, not living in the same town with her for so long. But Rick, as funny as these things are, they're all minor. Amy's never in her life messed up on something that really counted."

Rick looked over at the sad face of his sister-in-law and took a deep breath. "Maybe she hasn't, but it certainly wasn't for a lack of trying," he said deliberately.

Marsha stared over at his sober face in astonishment. "What did Amy nearly screw up?" she asked.

"Us. Her and me," Rick said. "I'm surprised Amy never told you about it."

Marsha shrugged. "I was going through my divorce about the time you two were working together that summer, and I overheard Mother telling her once not to say anything to me and add to my worries. That may be why she never said anything to me about it. What happened?"

Rick's face reflected remembered pain. "She thought I was a philanderer," he said flatly.

"You're kidding!" Marsha laughed. "Why, you're the last man on earth who would do that to her!"

"Thank you for the vote of confidence," Rick replied, transferring Danny to his shoulder. "Oh, it was more than that. She thought that since she's so brilliant, she would never be able to satisfy me as a woman, which of course is ridiculous. So she broke it off."

"I can't believe that Amy would make a mistake like that," Marsha murmured.

"Well, she did, and if it hadn't been for the intervention of a very dear friend, I guess she'd still be working herself into an early spinsterhood and I'd be partying every night trying to forget her. That error in judgment on her part almost cost us a future together."

176

Error in judgment. So Amy too was capable of an error in judgment about the man she loved. Biting her lip, Marsha turned troubled eyes on Rick. "But how do you know if you're making an error like that?" she asked as she clenched her fists in her lap.

Rick looked with knowing eyes at his sister-in-law. "Want to tell Uncle Rick about it?" he asked.

"I may as well," Marsha said, shrugging. "I was going to talk to Amy, since I thought she never made serious errors in judgment like I do."

"Well, she might very well have had good advice for you," Rick said. "It's usually people's own lives that they manage to mess up. So what's up?"

"Did Amy tell you that Ward asked me to marry him?" Marsha asked. Rick nodded. "And that I'd said yes?" Rick nodded again. Marsha took a deep breath. "Well, I tried to break it off, but Ward wouldn't let me. I was in his office this afternoon and, honestly, I wasn't snooping, but I found a letter of resignation from his teaching post out in New Mexico. Rick, he quit his job just like Jerry used to do!"

Rick raised a single eyebrow and shifted Danny to his other shoulder. "Don't you think there just might be an explanation?"

"I—I don't know," Marsha replied. "At least I don't think so. The letter was pretty clear."

"So what did Ward say when you asked him about it?"

"I haven't asked him about it," Marsha said. "I didn't want him to lie to me about it."

Rick looked positively exasperated. "You mean you haven't even asked the poor man for an explanation? Good grief, Marsha, you're even quicker to convict him on the basis of circumstantial evidence than Amy was me. And this is the second time you've done it to him. Don't you think you're making a mistake?"

"Damn it, Rick, that's the whole point! That's all I've ever done! First I fall for Jerry, then Jack. And now Ward —is he all right or is he just another loser? Do you honestly think I could go out and choose a decent man?"

"I don't see why not," Rick said calmly. "All right. You were just a kid when you fell for Jerry, and even Amy admits that he had you all fooled at first with all his charm."

"But then I turned around and started going with another loser," Marsha pointed out.

"Yes, but you were on the rebound from your lousy marriage, and anyone with two cents to rub together would have looked good to you at that point. Two years ago you were in no shape to make any kind of discriminating decision about anyone. But you haven't dated much since that fiasco and you've gotten over your divorce and you've grown up a whole hell of a lot in the last two years, so I think that you certainly are in a good position to choose a life's partner. You love the man, don't you?"

Marsha nodded, her eyes filling with tears. "I love him but I'm just not sure about him," she said. "Those letters really threw me."

"So go to him and ask him. Tell him your problem. But do it with confidence, Marsha. Honestly, your judgment is no better or worse than anyone else's. You just have to learn to trust it." Rick patted the diapered bottom of his son. "How about that? The little fellow zonked out on me while I was preaching to you!"

Marsha wiped the tears from her eyes and looked at her watch. "Damn, it's nearly midnight," she said. "I guess I better wait until morning."

Rick shook his head. "No, go on over there and put the poor man out of his misery," he said as he stood up, cradling his son on his shoulder.

178

"Thanks, Rick," Marsha said as she picked up her wallet and keys and reached up on her tiptoes to kiss Rick's cheek. "I'm glad Amy married you."

"I'm glad she did, too, at least most of the time," Rick said as they both laughed.

Marsha drove straight to Ward's house, praying that he would still be awake. She wanted to get this settled one way or the other tonight. Rick was right. She had convicted Ward for the second time, without giving him a chance to explain, and she at least owed him the chance to make an explanation. And she did need to learn to trust her own judgment. If Amy could make a mistake like that and learn from it, then so could she.

Marsha pulled up in the driveway of Ward's house, finding the front porch light on and the front door open. A van was parked in front of the house, and as she got out of the car a huge young man got out of the back of the van and walked up the sidewalk. Marsha shrank back, frightened momentarily, but she realized that if the door was open then at least someone in the house was aware of the man's presence. She walked up to the front door and let herself into the house, wandering out to the family room where Katy stood, her face wreathed in a smile, dressed in jeans and holding Bree in her arms. Ward stood beside her, a stern expression on his face as he glowered at the young man who had followed Marsha into the house.

"Marsha, I'm so glad you're here!" Katy said. "Tom, I'd like you to meet Marsha Walsh. She's the midwife who took care of me that night and she's engaged to Ward. Marsha, this is Tom Ingalls, Bree's father."

No wonder Ward's so sour, Marsha thought.

Tom extended a huge paw for Marsha to shake. "Katy tells me you were just great with her that night," he said.

"Thank you. We missed you that evening," Marsha

179

said pointedly, thinking of all the heartache that this young man had caused poor Katy.

Tom had the grace to look chagrined. "Miss Walsh, since you're going to marry Katy's brother I'll tell you the same thing I told him. If there was any way that I could undo the year of suffering I've put Katy through, I would gladly do it. I made a serious mistake when I left Katy, and I know that I hurt her. I intend to spend the rest of my life making up for what I put her through."

Marsha's cynical thoughts were mirrored on her face. "Please, Miss Walsh, you and Mr. Sentell have to believe me! Haven't you ever made a mistake?" Tom cried.

Marsha glanced over at Ward and shrugged. What could she say? She had made so many, and tonight she might almost have made another! Ward's face did not soften, but his eyes betrayed his uncertainty.

"Ward, Marsha, Tom has asked me to marry him," Katy said softly. "I can forgive him this last year because I love him."

Ward bent down and kissed Katy's cheek. "You're a generous woman." Then he stood squarely in front of Tom and looked up into Tom's face, speaking quietly yet firmly to the young man. "My sister may be able to forgive you for the past year, but I'm not so generous. If I ever, *ever* hear that you've made Katy unhappy again, I personally will come after you with a pistol, since you're too damn big to beat the hell out of. Do you understand?"

"Y—yes, sir," Tom stammered, not doubting that Ward meant every word. He picked up Katy's suitcase and carried it out to the van.

"Katy, honey, are you absolutely sure that you want to go with him?" Ward asked anxiously.

Katy nodded her head. "Yes, I am," she said firmly. "I

can sense the change in him since last year. He's grown up."

"I hope you're right," Ward said as he picked up Katy's other suitcase and followed her out to the van. He came back inside alone, his shoulders slumping dejectedly. "I have my doubts about her going with him, but there was no stopping her."

"She's a more forgiving woman than I could be, but I think maybe she will be all right," Marsha said as the van roared away into the night. "He didn't have to come back, you know." And who am I to criticize anyone else for making a mistake? she added to herself.

"What was that?" Ward asked.

Marsha shook her head. "Nothing." She sat down on the couch and picked up a throw pillow.

"What are you doing here at this late hour?" Ward asked. "I thought we had agreed to talk in the morning."

"Why did you resign from your job?" Marsha demanded.

"How did you know about that?" Ward asked.

"I knocked over a file on your desk and the first paper I picked up was a carbon of your resignation," she explained. "Then I read the letter from the University accepting the resignation. Why, Ward?"

"Didn't you read any of the other letters?" Ward asked, amusement in his eyes.

"No, I didn't!" she replied, horrified.

"Too bad," he said. "You would have saved us both a lot of misery. Marsha, an old colleague of mine, a woman named Wanda Shipley, has offered me a job, a full-time research job, at the Institute of Marine Science." Ward sat down and took Marsha's hand. "I already had another job when I resigned. It will mean no more teaching, ever again. I want that job a whole bunch, Marsha."

181

"You mean you already have another job?" Marsha asked, too relieved to take in any of the other.

"Of course I do! I would never quit one good job unless I already had another one lined up. Good jobs are hard to come by."

"How long do you plan to keep it?" Marsha asked warily.

"Well, since it's taken me nearly three years to land it and it's exactly what I want to do with myself for the rest of my life, I made damned sure they have a good retirement policy," he replied as Marsha breathed yet another sigh of relief. Ward got up and put his hands into his pockets, staring at Marsha with hurt in his eyes. "Why did you automatically assume the worst about me?" he asked. "This is the second time you've done it, you know. First with Katy, now with this job thing. It's like you expect me to mess up somehow."

"I guess that's because *I* do," Marsha admitted quietly.

"Why?" Ward asked, anguish in his voice.

Marsha swallowed back tears. "Because I've been attracted to a string of losers and I'm scared to death that you're going to turn out to be another one," she said as two tears escaped her eyes and ran down her cheeks. "First I married Jerry—I told you about him. Then I dated a guy named Jack. He turned out to be a professional gigolo. I'm scared, Ward. I'm afraid to trust my judgment about you."

Ward exhaled the breath he had been holding and sat back down beside her. "Don't you think I feel exactly the same way?" he asked softly.

"You do?" Marsha asked with astonishment. "Why?"

"Why do you think?" Ward asked. "I chose a wife once and thought I had chosen the perfect one. Then my perfect wife left me and my perfect marriage blew up in

182

my face. How am I supposed to feel after making a mistake like that? I'm scared to death!"

Marsha took a deep breath and stared at Ward with new eyes. She had been so worried about her own lack of judgment about Ward that it had never occurred to her that he had similar doubts about her. And he certainly had every right to! She reached out and took Ward's hand. "I think we better talk about this," she said as she traced a pattern with a finger on the back of his wrist.

"I love you, Ward, but I'm far from the perfect wife you had before. My cooking has not improved any in the last month, and I still loathe housework, and my telephone rings at odd hours, and I have to get up and go. I still like to ride my bicycle after dark and I haven't given away my skates. I'll always do some dumb things and make some mistakes, because that's in my nature."

Ward leaned over and kissed her on the cheek. "You know, I've had perfection and found out that it wasn't all that perfect. I think I'd rather just love you. Tell me," he said, looking into her eyes, "would you ever leave me for another man?"

Marsha shook her head. "Have you worried about that?" she asked as Ward nodded ruefully. "Oh, Ward, I would never do that to you! I love you too much to leave you."

"Thank you," he said as he kissed her again, this time on her lips. "Now, as for me, I want you to be well aware that you're not getting perfection either." He stood up and paced the den floor slowly. "I snore. I have heard it from the best of sources that I'm quite noisy once I have nodded off."

Marsha nodded her head. "I had noticed," she admitted.

"And I hate housework as much as you do, if not more. As far as I'm concerned, I'd just as soon turn on a

183

big fan twice a year and blow away all the debris," he said. "And if you ever do get around to washing, you will need to dig out all my socks and underwear from under the bed where I have kicked them." He stopped and paced back toward Marsha.

"I don't smoke and I'm positively rude to those who do. I have been accused on more than one occasion of being slightly bossy—no, make that terribly bossy, and I always choose the worst possible time to fuss at someone. Katy has accused me of being the original mother hen, so I suppose it's true.

"But, Marsha, I'll always work and support you. I want you to have a career, but I'll always have a good job. I won't mooch off you and your family as Jerry did. In fact, if you're willing to move to Port Aransas, that job at the institute will probably be the last career change I make."

Marsha nodded. "I wouldn't mind moving and starting a practice down there," she said slowly. "There are bound to be patients in the area."

"And, Marsha, I'm not going to cheat on you like that other man did," Ward promised her. "I'm not perfect, but, Marsha, I'm no loser."

Marsha nodded, then jumped up and wrapped her arms around Ward's neck. "Oh, thank God! You're all right! You're really not another loser!" Her eyes glowed with joy as she reached up and pulled his head down, kissing him on the lips. "I can finally trust my own judgment!"

"And I can finally trust mine," Ward said as he picked her up and whirled her around the room. "We're going to be all right, Marsha," he said as he pulled her head close to his and kissed her forcefully. Marsha melted into his embrace, her love and her joy flowing from her lips to Ward's. He pulled her closer, holding her body tightly against his as he snaked his tongue around the sides of her mouth, drawing shivers of pleasure from her as she grasped him by the shirt and pulled him close.

Ward broke off the kiss and held Marsha away from him. "Are you sure?" he asked. "Are you very sure?"

Marsha nodded. "Now, I want you to be very sure," he continued. "I want you to see exactly what you're getting," he said as he sat Marsha down on the couch. Sauntering over to the record cabinet, he got out a record and set it on the turntable, adjusting the volume as "The Stripper" blared out of his speakers.

Marsha started to laugh as Ward started dancing with the rhythm of the music, unbuttoning his shirt and sliding out of it and throwing it into her lap. She knew exactly what she was getting this time. She was getting a lovable idiot! Ward grinned at her and bounced with the music, his naked chest and back gleaming in the lamplight. "Come on, honey, take off some more!" Marsha said as she clapped and whistled.

Ward unstrapped his watch and tossed it to her. "That ain't enough, babe," she called.

Smiling sensuously, Ward kicked off his tennis shoes one by one, never missing a beat with the music. Then he lowered the zipper on his jeans and tried to wiggle out of them, but the jeans fit him like a second skin and refused to budge. "That ain't getting it, honey!" Marsha hooted.

"You were better at this than I am," Ward complained as he stopped and lowered his jeans. Once divested of those, he pulled off his socks and slipped out of his underwear, his desire for her clearly evident in his naked state. "I'd never make it at La Bare," he teased as he tossed his Jockeys into her lap.

"I'd rather have you just the way you are," Marsha volunteered as she held out her arms to Ward. "I love you, you lovable klutz."

Ward sat down beside her on the couch, holding her by the shoulders as he drank of the sweetness of her lips. "Look who's calling who a klutz," he complained as he slid down on the soft shag carpet and pulled Marsha down beside him. "Why am I naked and you're not?"

"I wasn't performing tonight." Marsha laughed as Ward started to unbutton her blouse. "What's this?" he asked, fingering a small pasty glob on her blouse.

"Some of Danny's cereal," she said as Ward nuzzled her neck with his soft tongue.

"What were you doing over there?" Ward asked as he pushed her blouse off her shoulders and trailed his mouth down her collarbone, sending shivers of delight through Marsha.

"I wanted to talk to Amy but talked to Rick instead," she explained as she touched Ward's shoulders with her fingers. "He said to come and talk to you about your job, so I did."

"Smart man," Ward said as he unzipped Marsha's jeans. "Stand up."

Obediently Marsha stood up and Ward pushed the jeans down her body, his hands lingering on her shapely legs. Then he hooked his fingers into her panties and slid them down her legs, baring her body to his eager gaze. "You're so beautiful," Ward murmured as he drew her to him. "I'm going to make love to you right here, right now. I'm not even going to take the time to carry you to my bed."

"Oh, I love you, Ward," Marsha murmured as she snaked her arms around his neck and pulled him close, melting into the soft carpet, kissing him and touching him with all the love she felt for him. I can love this man, she thought as Ward took command of the kiss and parted her lips, probing and drinking of the sweetness

186

within. He's a winner. I can trust him. He's going to do right by me.

I can love her, Ward thought as he dipped his head and caressed her breast with his tongue, teasing it into a hard knot of desire as she twisted and moaned beneath him. She isn't going to desert me. She's going to be here with me always. I can give her all my love and she won't trample it. His lips traveled down the soft skin of her abdomen, touching and grazing the silky soft skin, then the light down that covered it. The feel of the soft, lightly scented skin on his lips aroused him to a searing, mindless passion. He wanted to touch her, to take her, to make her completely his own. Curbing his own wild desire, he continued to torment Marsha, delighting in the soft kitten noises she made deep in her throat.

"I need you, Ward," Marsha murmured as his lips continued to trace an erotic pattern on her soft waist and stomach, driving her desire into a mind-spinning spiral. Wanting to love him as he was loving her, she sat up and pushed him back into the carpet, covering his chest and stomach with soft, damp kisses, darting out her small pink tongue to caress the velvet skin of his chest and stomach and the soft brown hair that covered it. She let her lips drift lower, touching him intimately in the way that he loved so well. Not content to stop there, Marsha continued to kiss and caress her way down his body, touching and caressing his strong thighs, his calves, even his toes.

Ward pulled Marsha back up on top of him, running his hands across her breasts and down her body as he gazed up at the woman he loved so. Then his questing fingers crept lower and found her secret place and tormented it lovingly, sending shivers of delight down to Marsha's toes.

"You're ready," Ward said a moment later as Marsha whimpered with pleasure. "Make love to me."

Delighted that Ward wanted her to take the initiative, Marsha moved over him and made them one, their bodies joining together in complete and trusting joy. I love him and I know that I can trust him, Marsha thought as Ward's body twisted beneath her. And he loves me and he isn't going to hurt me. Her loving thoughts giving way to actions, Marsha poured every bit of her love and her joy into her embrace, moving over Ward with sure, confident strokes, driving him further and further toward the brink of ecstasy. Her own tension building, Marsha moved faster and harder, lifting both herself and Ward to the highest realms of pleasure. As she could feel herself losing control, Ward exploded beneath her, his passion bursting forth in uncontrollable waves. Whimpering softly, Marsha let go with her own feelings, her finale erupting in dizzying spasms of pleasure.

"That was divine," Ward said a moment later as Marsha slid from him and curled up beside his warm, sweaty body. "Marsha, I love you so much!"

"I love you too," Marsha said as she snuggled against Ward. "And I'm so happy that I was right about you, that you're everything you seem to be."

"Well, we've made our share of mistakes, both of us, but that's over now."

"Yes, that's over. No more errors in judgment. No more mistakes—*mistakes!*" Marsha bolted upright and stared at Ward. "I forgot my birth control!"

"Uh-oh, something tells me our mistakes are only beginning," Ward said as he pulled Marsha back down beside him. "Well, don't worry about it. The chances of your getting pregnant from just this once are really pretty slim."

188

"But it's just the right time of the month for it to happen!" Marsha wailed.

"Will you calm down? I promise you, Marsha, you're not going to get pregnant from tonight."

"I bet I do," Marsha said.

"I bet you don't," Ward replied.

Marsha won the bet.

All-new
Candlelight Newsletter

An exceptional, *free* offer awaits readers of Dell's incomparable Candlelight Ecstasy and Supreme Romances.

Subscribe to our all-new CANDLELIGHT NEWSLETTER and you will receive—at absolutely no cost to you—exciting, exclusive information about today's finest romance novels and novelists. You'll be part of a select group to receive sneak previews of upcoming Candlelight Romances, well in advance of publication.

You'll also go behind the scenes to "meet" our Ecstasy and Supreme authors, learning firsthand where they get their ideas and how they made it to the top. News of author appearances and events will be detailed, as well. And contributions from the Candlelight editor will give you the inside scoop on how she makes her decisions about what to publish—and how *you* can try your hand at writing an Ecstasy or Supreme.

You'll find all this and more in Dell's CANDLELIGHT NEWSLETTER. And best of all, *it costs you nothing*. That's right! It's Dell's way of thanking our loyal Candlelight readers and of adding another dimension to your reading enjoyment.

Just fill out the coupon below, return it to us, and look forward to receiving the first of many CANDLELIGHT NEWSLETTERS—overflowing with the kind of excitement that only enhances our romances!

Return to: DELL PUBLISHING CO., INC.   B290A
        Candlelight Newsletter • Publicity Department
        245 East 47 Street • New York, N.Y. 10017

Name_____

Address_____

City_____

State_____Zip_____

Candlelight
Ecstasy Romances™

$1.95 each